# *Heath*

## Hathaway House, Book 8

# Dale Mayer

### Books in This Series:

HEATH: HATHAWAY HOUSE, BOOK 8
Dale Mayer
Valley Publishing Ltd.

Copyright © 2019

This is a work of fiction. Names, characters, places, brands, media, and incidents are either the product of the author's imagination or are used fictitiously. Any resemblance to actual events, locales, or persons, living or dead, is entirely coincidental.

ISBN-13: 978-1-773363-80-6
Print Edition

# About This Book

Welcome to Hathaway House, a heartwarming and sweet military romance series from USA TODAY best-selling author Dale Mayer. Here you'll meet a whole new group of friends, along with a few favorite characters from Heroes for Hire. Instead of action, you'll find emotion. Instead of suspense, you'll find healing. Instead of romance, ... oh, wait. ... There is romance—of course!

*Welcome to Hathaway House. Rehab Center. Safe Haven. Second chance at life and love.*

Overjoyed at his transfer to Hathaway House, Heath Jorgenson is anxious to maximize his potential and to get better from the multiple injuries that sidelined him. But rest is necessary for recovery, and Heath's body won't give him any. Even when he buckles under and accepts the need for drugs, his body rejects them. And all the determination in the world won't matter when your own body is working against you.

Just when he's about to give up, respite comes from the unlikeliest of sources. The sound of the cleaning lady slowly and methodically washing the hall floor outside his room lulls him to sleep and allows him to see some of the progress he's desperate for.

Hailee Cisco is grateful for the part-time job of washing floors at Hathaway House. Sure, it isn't glamorous, but it's honest work, and, along with her other job, it's enough to pay the bills—of which Hailee has many. When Dani, the heart of and the partial owner of Hathaway House, offers Hailee a full-time job, Hailee is delighted at the chance to cut back to just one job.

Until she realizes that her change in hours has an unintended impact on Heath's sleep patterns …

# Chapter 1

HEATH HANKERSON HAD fought his surgeon hard to sign off on his transfer to Hathaway House. As he was healing at a tremendous rate, the surgeon had finally been persuaded to let Heath sign on with somebody else, and that had let him take the open bed at Hathaway House.

"I've heard a lot of good things about Hathaway House," Dr. Macklin said. "I'm surprised you got in. But then, the fact that you did means maybe this is where you need to go."

"I think it means exactly that," Heath said in a quiet voice. "I want this opportunity. I've heard some pretty decent things myself."

"A lot of other good rehab centers are around the country though," Dr. Macklin said, as he studied Heath's face with care. "You could probably pick and choose."

"That's exactly it. And I have done exactly that. And I'm choosing Hathaway House."

"In that case, there's nothing more to talk about," the doctor said. "You're progressing well, and I would like to get regular updates. We've done a lot of surgeries, so it'll take quite a bit of time to recover. At this point I have no idea how well you'll do, but I'm hoping for a full recovery."

"I know it's up to me now."

"I'll write up detailed notes for the physio team there to continue the work you've been doing."

"I'd appreciate that," Heath said.

"Wouldn't hurt you to send me an email every once in a while too," Dr. Macklin said. And then he laughed. "I still get emails from patients I treated twenty years ago."

"That's because you care," Heath said with a grin.

"I do. It's not easy. We see people in pretty rough shape when they initially come in. We do the best we can, and sometimes it works, but sometimes it doesn't. At a certain point, the medical technology can only do so much for you. In this case, you've done pretty well though. Now it's up to the physio and to your own will to be better."

Heath nodded, and, just as he slowly moved out of the office, Dr. Macklin called out behind him.

"Do you have a specific reason for going to Hathaway House?"

Heath turned, looked at the doctor, and smiled. "Well, Houston was always home. I don't have any family left, but something is drawing me back there. As for why Hathaway outside of the location ..." He pondered for a moment and then said, "I guess the only answer I really have is just this gut feeling about it."

The doctor looked at him thoughtfully for a long moment, then nodded, and said, "Sometimes, as you know, the gut feeling is all we have to go on. In this case, I think it's an excellent call."

As Heath made his way to the elevator, he hoped the doctor was right. Heath had gone over the Hathaway House website with a fine-tooth comb and had talked to several people that he'd known to get help there. Some had tried to get in and had been refused because no bed had been available in time. On the other hand, a couple guys had come out of their treatment there and had glowing praises.

At the end of the day, all Heath personally had to go on was that gut feeling of his. He could only hope it would work out in his favor this time. He didn't have a whole lot of options left.

HAILEE CISCO WORKED her way down the hallway, moving the mop slowly across the white-tiled floor. As she did, she pulled the bucket behind her. It was two in the morning, and she was just about done with her cleaning shift, a job she had just started about a month ago. Hathaway House was one of those places that needed to be maintained and kept absolutely crisp and clean. A lot of sick men and women were here, and nobody could afford infections.

The fact that a large animal center was also downstairs just added to the need to be extra careful about cleanliness. She was all for the animals, but she knew that they added another level of possible contamination for the humans here. These patients couldn't afford that. Their bodies were weak and already struggling.

So she worked hard. She took care and pride in her job, even though it was a job that she hadn't ever considered doing. Right now, it was a balm to her soul and a soothing hug to her very stressed-out body. She felt like she'd walked through a war herself to get where she was. Of course it certainly didn't have the same kind of impact that a lot of these men—and women—had gone through. But every night that she came through here, she took a moment or so to reflect and used the cleaning as a way for her own soul to get back on track.

She focused hard and kept her head down while she

worked and cleaned the hallway. As she did, she eviscerated the stain from her body, her soul, and her emotions. She was a long way from being whole, but she owed Dani a lot for giving her this chance. Dani had tried hard to provide Hailee with a different job, one that dealt with more people to take her out of her shell, but Hailee couldn't handle it yet. She couldn't interact with people. She couldn't bear to feel the hurt that came with making friends or the pain that came with trusting the wrong person or the betrayal that sometimes happened between family members and friends.

Automatically she pushed the mop into the big bucket of water and pulled it out slightly, then used the ringer to take most of the moisture off the heavy twisted cotton ropes. She had never used a mop like this before. But it worked well, and that's all she cared about. She dropped it to the floor and sent it slowly across the floor.

*Swish. Swish. Swish.*

Back into the water, rinse, wash, and repeat. She worked slowly but steadily. She knew she was avoiding the far corner, as she did every night. She was hoping that maybe this time she wouldn't hear what she'd listened to every other night. Something that tore her apart, something that made her own heart bleed. The patients' stories that came out of this place were enough to make anybody cry.

When she had first heard a man behind the doors sobbing quietly to himself, thinking that he was alone, it tore her insides apart. Not only for his pain that she could do nothing about, but also for invading his privacy. She had no name for him, and maybe it was better that way because it hurt enough even without a personal connection. Then again all of it hurt. Which defeated her ultimate purpose.

She didn't come here to be torn apart further. She came

here to heal. It had been Dani's suggestion, and they had been friends for a long time. So she'd trusted her friend, who seemed to understand healing at a whole other level, and here Hailee was.

Hailee had worked at one of the large warehouse stores in the city. She'd often arranged for supplies to be delivered to Hathaway House. Yet again that also wasn't what she wanted to do. She was an accountant by profession, and somehow she had ended up working on the warehouse floor and then finally walked away from that too. Sometimes one had to start fresh. You could only hang on to the pain for so long before it was absolutely mandatory to make a change. Dani had offered Hailee this lifeline, and she'd taken it.

It was as if cleaning here would help her clean her soul. Dani had reassured Hailee that she had nothing to be ashamed of since her soul held nothing but goodness, and life was just sometimes contrary like that. But Hailee hadn't managed to let her past go. She hadn't managed to find peace the same way Dani had. Her friend was so happy. It was such a joy to watch Dani every time Aaron came home. She just bounced full of life.

Hailee wanted to feel that same joy again.

Hailee knew Dani's wedding was in the planning stages, but it would be a long way away. And, for Hailee, she could only hope that maybe she'd be lucky and be invited. Hopefully she'd still be working here. She took several more steps, rinsed her mop, and whooshed again. Then she slowly worked down the long main hallway.

She loved working at the rehab center. It was an incredible place. It hadn't taken even a few weeks of being here to see that. She was astonished at how warm and caring everyone in the center was. She had previously known about it and had realized that anything Dani was involved in had a lot of heart. But it was one thing when you're on the outside hearing about what happened here at the center. It was an entirely different thing to actually see the emotions, the people, and the heart beating in this place.

*Or the pain …*

As soon as that thought popped into her mind, she shook her head and started scrubbing the floor that didn't need to be cleaned yet again. She wouldn't dwell on the pain. There was always pain. And, if she couldn't help herself, she sure couldn't help anybody else. And she was a long way away from helping herself.

She carried on mopping the floor, moving her Beware of Wet Floor sign as she went. Even though it was calm and quiet in these early morning hours, it didn't mean that people weren't walking through the hallways. Nurses were moving from room to room, taking care of patients as needed. Hailee gripped her mop tighter. As long as she wasn't personally involved with anyone here, she could handle being here. Staying detached was the only way she could deal with doctors after what she'd been through.

It was a miracle she could do even that.

# Chapter 2

HAILEE HADN'T THOUGHT it possible that she would end up at a place like this, but Dani had been adamant that her center was different. That not just the patients healed here.

Hailee sighed, knowing that the last door was coming up. This was a short hallway off the main one, and, as she came to the end, she knew she would reach the door where every night she cringed—or softly cried with him—at the pain eking from that room.

It wasn't because she wanted to avoid it but because she knew she couldn't. It was almost a penance, as if somebody needed to witness his pain so he could release it and let it go. *Or maybe it was her own penance.* Regardless she knew it sounded foolish, and she didn't understand it herself because he would probably be horrified if he thought someone could hear him. And it was definitely a man's voice; she avoided reading his name on the medical file in the box affixed to his door to confirm that. She'd yet to have anything to do with any of the patients. But then, part of that was due to working a night shift. A position she'd asked for.

She kept her head down and worked away at scrubbing the floor. This was her last pass, and, after this little bit, she was done. She went to the far end and worked her way backward.

When she got to *the* door, she smiled in joy. The room was silent. No signs of someone struggling on the other side. She walked, moved, cleaned, scrubbed, and did her penance for her own soul's sake tonight. As she was just about done, she heard it start again. Her breath caught in the back of her throat. He was crying about his pain. But in many ways it was about her pain too. He was crying the sobs that she couldn't let out, the sobs that were deep within herself. She stayed where she was, her head bowed, as she wished him well, wishing him a more peaceful night. Even though he cried, surely tonight it seemed his pain was less.

Satisfied with that little bit of hope, she gathered her bucket and headed back to the utility closet in the laundry room, where she could clean the mops and put away her cleaning supplies. Another night done. And hopefully another little brick of goodness to build a wall to survive the new world she lived in. It wasn't fair, and it wasn't easy, but it's the one that she had. Once people got their minds wrapped around their current reality and could see their way forward, they could do so much more than when avoiding that reality.

But, of course, the problem often was people got hung up on where they were and couldn't get to where they were going. In those moments, it seemed like the distance was so damn far that they couldn't find a way to get there. Yet, in fact, it didn't need to be that way at all. People could cross any amount of distance without any issues. They just had to believe in it and put in the effort. That's the most laborious and time-consuming part. But it was all about taking that first step.

Hailee had attended yoga and meditation sessions because they were both so darn crucial for stress relief. And one of the things she loved was when they were told to visualize themselves in a cloud, where the only thing they could see was a little bit of a space where they stood. And then they were told to take a little step forward into the unknown, into the unseen. It was amazing to listen to people calling out that they were falling and were too scared to take action because they couldn't see what was in front of them.

And, of course, that was the lesson. To trust that a step would be there, that you would be okay, and that, as soon as you put your foot out there, another step would form under it, so that you wouldn't fall. But so many people struggled with that concept. Hailee had used it many times for herself, trying to get through what she needed to get through in life. The last few years hadn't been easy. Yet she had not only survived but she'd also become a much better person for it. She smiled at that as she returned her cleaning supplies at the end of her shift.

Hathaway House might be perfect for the patients here, but it was the right place for Hailee too.

HEATH LAY ONCE again on his bed and stared up at the dark sky just outside his window. It seemed like darkness was his friend these days. Or maybe an enemy. It gave him the privacy of being alone, but with it came the most incredible nightmares and the most horrific images that he never wanted to see again. There should be a way to stop it. He knew that all kinds of meditations and drugs and things could deal with it, but, in his heart of hearts, he knew that part of the problem was he didn't want them to stop. Because, as long as he relived these memories, he never forgot his friends who blew up beside him.

He lived. They died. But, as long as he remembered them, they weren't forgotten.

Two of his friends were scheduled to head back to the US with him two days later for their leave. Both of them were excited. They had girlfriends they were heading home to. Heath, on the other hand, didn't. He was the only unattached one. They'd been joking and laughing when he drove too close to the shoulder, and the truck hit an IED. He'd taken part of the blast, but his friends had lost their lives.

And, every night, he drove that same damn road, wrenching the wheel to prevent the accident because now he knew what would happen when he hit that shoulder. But there was no forgiveness. There was no change. There was no going back. There was no fixing this, and every time he thought about his best friends and their girlfriends and their bright futures, it always came back to the same questions: *Why me? Why was I the one to survive? Why was I the one to stay here and to suffer through all this pain and the guilt? Why couldn't they have lived, even if they'd lost their legs? Their women would have loved them regardless. Their families wouldn't have cared as long as their sons, brothers were still there to love and had something to look forward to.*

But it was just him, staring up at the ceiling and the lovely apparatus that came with these beds. He hoped he was past his need to use the hoists, but he certainly had initially.

Heath had heard the doctors talking about mental blocks and resistance and all kinds of other psychobabble. Heath wanted to ignore the docs. He wanted to say they were full of crap, but he knew, deep in his soul, what they were talking about. His own guilt was eating at him and was keeping him from functioning as he should. He wasn't even sure he cared. What he wanted to do was find a way to be a better person, so he didn't ever have to live with this horrible guilt again. Yet the sin was there, the terrible mistake, and he knew it would never go away. And that's the way of it. It was his penance.

His life goal now was to live the best life he could to make up for his friends' deaths. Heath should have been the one who died. That he didn't was something he would have to live with for the rest of his life.

He closed his eyes, hoping that maybe this time he could sleep. Sleep was necessary for healing. He also knew that the docs thought Heath needed to continue seeing the psychologist. The psychologist felt that Heath needed to talk more. And he needed them to just go away and to leave him the hell alone.

The black abyss was one that he rightly belonged in. He shouldn't even be here, shouldn't be taking up a bed. He didn't even know how he'd really come to be here. In one of his more positive moments he'd applied to a bunch of places, and, sure, this had been one of them, but he hadn't really thought he'd get in. When the acceptance letter came, he'd been given a bunch more paperwork, and he hadn't cared either way but figured he'd started something so needed to carry it through. He'd signed them and passed them on. Next thing he knew, he was transferred here. But it hadn't really settled in as to where and to what he'd been transferred to.

As he lay here hating himself and the world he lived in, he could hear the cleaning lady go by—every night as regular as clockwork. He heard the *swish* of the mop as she dropped it back into the bucket, trying to be quiet but failing. The requirements of her job necessitated some noise. There was something about the mundaneness of her actions, knowing that she was out there and that he, therefore, wasn't alone.

Yet, after his nightmares every night, seeing his two buddies blown up once more, his tears welled up. He always tried to hold them off, but it was hard. Deep down, he silently wished that somebody could know he was in such pain. Yet that was foolish because, in his rational mind, he didn't want anybody to know. However, she was a silent witness to his own pain. He hated it, but it was a connection he needed, only hadn't known it until she started her nightly ritual. It was just one more thing in Heath's life that was so wrong.

And still, to hear her out there, swishing back and forth, he'd often imagined what she must look like. He figured she had to be at least in her fifties and gray-haired. He wondered if she'd left a half-dozen kids at home. Maybe even grand-children? Perhaps she had a husband who was retired. Heath didn't know why it was easier to imagine her as older. Maybe it was the thoroughness with which she cleaned everything.

He could tell time by her movements too. Every night it took her exactly twenty minutes to get to his door. The tears would have already started and now stopped when he finally heard her mop. That sound always made him hold back the tears a little bit better. He hated it, and yet he waited for it. Sometimes teary-eyed. Sometimes sleepy-eyed. He wondered now if he woke up just in time to hear her. He often considered opening the door to see her. Not to embarrass her by any means and not to worry her or scare her, but just for that connection to somebody who had obviously heard his pain and was still here, day in and day out.

Maybe to know he hadn't scared her away.

Heath never cried in the morning. He never cried during the day, even after Shane put him through the paces. That new guy, Jeff, was supposed to be just as wickedly good too. Or wickedly bad, depending on your viewpoint. Heath seriously hurt after his physical therapy sessions, but Shane kept saying that Heath was getting better, getting stronger. He would just smile and nod, knowing Shane was full of crap.

Because Heath wasn't getting any better; no way he could get better. Who could possibly want him to get better? He held too much pain, too much horror, too much of everything. He wasn't suicidal; he just wished that life had been a whole lot fairer and had taken him and had left his friends to live their lives and their dreams with their partners who cared for them. Heath was alone and had always been alone. He knew nothing else. The light in his life had been his two buddies. He'd been an orphan, and nobody else had been in his life like they were. They'd known each other since they first enlisted. He shook his head, trying to figure it out.

"You've been there with me for the longest period of time that I've ever known anyone," he whispered. "But still you were taken from me." And more like a parent who'd lost their child or a brother who'd lost his siblings, Heath had been left, bereft and alone. And he hated it. He'd do damn-near anything to not be this way anymore. *Bereft. Alone.* Anything *but* go out to meet and to enjoy the entire community of other broken people in this rehab facility.

Because to acknowledge them was to accept himself.

## Chapter 3

HAILEE SAT IN the hallway, holding her coffee, taking a breather before she started work at her second job of the day. She'd come in from her low-level bookkeeping job in town—where she holed up in her office with her head down and with no one to distract her—straight to Hathaway House. This was her life, and it sucked, but each was honest work, and each brought in its own paycheck.

Her phone buzzed with a text. She smiled at her lawyer's message. It was simple and didn't say anything really. But the message **Making progress** made her smile. He was trying to reduce her medical bills from Jacob's intensive treatments. That Jacob hadn't made it through didn't matter to the debt-collection laws or to the hospital. It didn't matter that she'd struggled to keep food on the table while her infant son had struggled to take each breath.

He'd been gone a year now. A year of deep soul searching, working multiple jobs, and fighting for a greatly reduced hospital bill that would set her free and clear within her own lifetime. Her lawyer also considered going after the company that had laid her off when her son's health issues had hit hard at the company's health coverage. Of course they didn't fire her. They found a way to make her position redundant.

But the hospital bill was the more important issue. She sighed. And could only hope that this nightmare would be over soon.

Voices reached her around the corner from the direction of the offices.

"Did we get a new cleaning lady?"

Hailee stiffened with worry. She couldn't see who was speaking and didn't recognize the voice, but dozens of staff members were here, so it could be anyone. "Hi, Anna. Yes, a friend of mine is cleaning for us. Yes," Dani said, her voice easily sliding down the hallway. "Problems?"

"No," Anna said. "I was just commenting on the fact that everything seemed so clean, and a lemon scent is in the air when I come in first thing in the morning now."

"That'll be Hailee," Dani said. "She loves lemon. As long as nobody complains about it, then I'm happy to let her use it."

"No, it's quite nice," Anna said, her footsteps clipping across the floor as she walked. She seemed to pause and then asked, "Do you know her well?"

"I do. She has gone through some rough times lately. This job isn't one that she would normally do. I have a great need for an accountant, and she is one, but I haven't quite convinced her to come here full-time."

"She's an accountant, but instead she's doing the cleaning?" Anna asked in surprise.

Hailee winced. She hadn't asked Dani to keep that to herself, but Hailee was a reserved and private person and wouldn't want others talking behind her back. Although it was human nature, she'd like to avoid their curiosity if possible.

Dani added slowly, "And I'd appreciate it if you don't pass that on. We all have to do what we need to do for whatever reason we feel is right."

Prophetic words. Hailee smiled as she sipped her coffee. Dani was a wise woman.

"I don't have a problem not talking about her," Anna said. "I'd love to meet her, but I don't ever see her. She's not here when I arrive, and she must show up after I've left."

"That's the way she likes it too. Sometimes it takes time to adjust to being around people."

"Not sure cleaning on the night shift will do that," Anna said doubtfully.

"No, but we have to do what we need to do in our own time frame."

"That seems to be one of the Hathaway House mottos here," Anna said. "Everybody makes progress in their own way."

Hailee peeked around the corner.

Anna stepped out of Dani's office into the hallway, then stopped, and, with a big smile, turned back to face Dani again. "Speaking of which, I was down with Stan. Did you see that new cat he's got down there?"

"A new cat?"

"If that's what it is," she said. "It's huge. I have no clue. But it's missing a full back leg, like it was taken right off at the hip, but it's got the temperament of a teddy bear."

"Wow," Hailee muttered. She wished she could take a look. She had yet to be in the veterinarian clinic. They had their own cleaning staff.

"I hadn't heard," Dani said. "I may take a look at this guy myself."

"You should," Anna said, now standing in Dani's doorway. "She's huge. As in seriously huge."

"Is she really?"

Anna stopped, tossed her head to the side a little bit as

she considered the question, then nodded. "She definitely has an extra pouch on her. I think she must have had a litter, and she's holding some of that belly weight," she said with a laugh. "A common complaint all mothers have."

"Generally the animal world doesn't care about it though," Dani said. "It's just us crazy human females."

"Isn't that the truth," Anna said with a chuckle. "Anyway, I'll talk to you tomorrow."

Anna tossed Dani a bright smile as she headed down the hallway, away from Hailee.

On that note, before Dani stepped out and realized that Hailee had heard them, Hailee got up and headed off to start her shift.

WHEN HEATH WOKE up again, gasping, his breath seizing in his chest and his body completely covered in sweat, he didn't need to check his clock to know that it would be right around two a.m. He waited for the sounds outside in the hallway to slowly penetrate through the massive din of screams in back of his mind. He could hear his friends screaming over and over and over again. Some cruel twist of fate had this exact same moment frozen in time being relived in his nightmares.

It could have been ten minutes earlier, or it could have been ten minutes later, but it was always when the truck blew up, and he could hear the screams and roars and then the deafening silence. Except the silence was broken by his own sobs. From his friends, there was nothing. Not a sound. And that was worse than anything.

He'd once again be laying there on the desert ground,

staring up at the sky, and hoping that he was wrong, hoping that they were just knocked unconscious. But he already knew that they were gone. Such an emptiness resided inside his soul. The only brothers he'd ever known, the only real friends he'd ever had, the only people who had ever given a damn about him were gone. Worse, he'd been responsible.

He didn't quite understand what had happened, but he knew that Shawn had reached over and grabbed the wheel. They were joking and laughing, and he'd done it as a joke, but his movement had driven the truck to the shoulder of the road. Heath had been too surprised to react fast enough. He *should* have jerked the steering wheel back faster to keep them on the roadway. But he hadn't, and then he had no time to respond.

It was just over.

It was becoming quite a habit now, but, as he lay here, his body tense in the cool air and slowly drying as the sweat evaporated around him, he could hear the sounds he expected. The *swish-swish* of the mop going back and forth across the tiled floors. He smiled and settled back into his bed—almost as if hearing her helped him to stay grounded in this world and a long way away from all the nightmares and the cries around him.

Comforted by the sounds proving she was out there, he closed his eyes and let the repetitive sounds, moving back and forth, ease his soul, bringing him back to the reality of where he lived now. This was his life. And, even as the screams faded, the sound of the mop became louder and louder. It was a comfort; it was a reassurance. It was a connection to another living soul.

And, more than that, it fired up his curiosity about her. Whoever the poor woman was, the last thing she needed was some scary-ass dude like himself opening the door and frightening her. He could get up and open the door at any time; he knew that, but just something about the mystery of her kept him glued into the bed. He closed his eyes and let sleep take him once again.

## Chapter 4

WHEN HAILEE SHOWED up for work the next evening at eight, she was surprised to see Dani still working in her office. Dani looked up and called her over. "I hope you didn't stay late for my sake," Hailee said worriedly. "Am I not doing a decent job?"

Dani looked at her in surprise. "Oh my," she said, "you're doing a wonderful job. And several people have commented about the fresh lemon scent."

"Is that okay?" Hailee asked, still worried if her friend and boss had waited for her intentionally.

"It's more than okay," Dani said warmly. "Stop being so worried."

"It's hard not to be," she said. "At least now."

"It'll be fine. Just chill."

"Got it," Hailee said, laughing. "And, if there's no problem, I need to get to work." And, with that, she took off. Sometimes she headed to the laundry area to see how that was going. She came in and helped out in that department a few hours a week. She was totally okay to do whatever was needed, and some weeks it was a little more than others.

As she walked into the laundry area, Dennis from the kitchen brought in another big load of kitchen towels. She grinned at him. "You know what? You guys almost dominate the laundry these days. Sometimes way more kitchen laundry here than bedding."

"Lots of people eating," he said. "Lots of cooking happening. Lots of kitchen towels. But we're nowhere near what the bedding or the linens are or the towels for the showers."

"Just seems like it," she said. She took the large hamper and wielded it toward one of the big machines and quickly filled one washer. She added in the soap as required, closed the door, and started it. When she turned, Dennis stood there, his hands on his hips, studying her.

"What's up?" she asked casually, as she walked over to the utility closet, where her mops and brooms and dustpans were. She would clean the kitchen and dining room area tonight. She turned toward him. "When does the dining room close?"

"Never, really," he said. "Drinks are always available for any of the patients. Are you gonna vacuum?"

She nodded. "I just thought I would start there a little earlier tonight."

"Go ahead," he said. "Are you doing the bathrooms too?"

She nodded. "I'll vacuum first and then hit up the bathrooms."

"Good enough," he said.

As he stepped back, she nudged the hamper at him. "Here you go. You can refill it. I will send another up with folded towels when that load's done."

He grabbed the hamper, grinned, and said, "It's nice to see a friendly face down here."

She stared at him in surprise. "Everybody is friendly here."

He shook his head. "Don't often see anybody in here. Most of the time, I put the laundry on myself."

"That's hardly needed," she said. "There's like four people doing laundry at this place every day."

"Yeah, but why add more work for other people if it's something you can do yourself?"

She nodded. "Well, I agree, but most people don't."

He shrugged. "But we," he said, pointing his finger at her and then him, "are not normal people."

"No, we aren't," she said with a smile. She watched as he disappeared, whistling, happy and cheerful as always. He was one of the most upbeat people she'd ever met. She used to be optimistic. She used to be bright and cheerful, but life had dealt her one too many blows, and she didn't even feel like she had the time or the effort anymore. And that was such a defeatist attitude.

On that note, she grabbed her commercial vacuum and headed up the service elevator to the dining room. With Dennis quickly moving chairs and tables for her, she got started. When she turned around, he was wiping down the tables and the tops of the condiment bottles with a cloth, then wiping down all the chair seats too. She smiled. "You make my job easy."

"You've got enough to do," he said. "At least a dozen public bathrooms are in this place."

She chuckled. "Hey, but I'm not doing the private bathrooms, so it's much better."

He rolled his eyes at that. "If you need a hand in the bathrooms, let me know."

She shook her head. "I'll lose my job. If we're too efficient, you'll cut my hours in half."

He frowned. "I don't want to do that."

She chuckled. "I'm kidding. You have lots of work to do for tomorrow yourself."

"Yep, but I'm waiting for somebody. We're seeing a movie in town. So, for fifteen to twenty minutes, I can do a little bit of extra work too." At that, he started refilling the salt and pepper shakers.

She left him to do his kitchen duties. She wasn't exactly sure what position he held, but he was everywhere, from the kitchen to the dining room to the laundry area. He was one of those guys just happy to lend a hand, and she wished more people were like him.

She headed to the bathrooms, gloves on and armed with lots of cleansers and her mop. She didn't mind doing the bathrooms. She had such a great sense of satisfaction when everything turned out sparkling clean. She moved steadily from one bathroom to the other. By the time midnight hit, she was damn-near done. But now it was time to start the floors. That always took her a couple hours.

She checked her watch and realized she was running a little bit behind. She headed back to the utility closet and switched out some of her cleansers. And then, with the mop and her bucket filled with hot water and the floor-cleaning solution, she started mopping on the main floor and then moved upward. It would take her over two hours tonight. It looked like the floors were dirtier than usual, which meant changing her bucket of water more often. But she was up for it. Every time she did this, she imagined each stroke cleaning the pain and sorrow of her own soul.

She moved steadily through the hallways, washing and scrubbing, moving the mop back and forth to a natural rhythm that seemed to ease something inside her. The routine movement and the sense of hard work, knowing that she was doing something necessary and in some way contributing to somebody else's healing, it all helped. Maybe that was good for her own soul too. She moved in a steady rhythmic motion, absolutely loving to see the clean floors as she moved backward down each hall. By the time she came around to the final hallway, she knew she was running almost half an hour behind. She headed down with a bucket of fresh water and started working on the floor.

She heard a sound. She stopped, frowned, and then softly called out, "Are you okay?"

A ghost of a voice answered, "No."

She immediately went to the door, knocked, and opened it slightly, poking her head around the corner into the dark room. "Do you want me to call a nurse?"

"Yes, please."

She immediately closed the door and raced to the closest nursing station. Tina was there. Hailee told her about the patient in the far room. Tina followed her and headed inside the room that Hailee had only ever stuck her head into once. She could hear their voices on the other side in the darkness. She hadn't actually seen the patient, but he needed somebody. Happy that she could help, Hailee picked up her mop and resumed working again.

By the time she finished, her soul was a little lighter, and she realized that, on a scale of one to ten today, she was running around an eight.

Considering she'd been working closer to the six or seven range every day for the last three weeks, this wasn't bad. But today, well, was a little bit better. She cleaned up her mop and put away her bucket, then headed back to check that she'd collected everything. She'd left her Wet Floor sign, and she snatched that up.

The door to *his* room opened. Tina walked out, smiled at Hailee, and said, "Thanks for calling me."

Hailee nodded slowly. "I didn't know what I heard. I felt terrible even knocking."

"In this specific case," Tina said, "it was the right thing to do."

"I'm glad to hear that," she said. "I really don't have much to do with any of the patients here, so I never really know."

"Not to worry," Tina said with a smile. She headed back to the nurse's station.

Hailee followed ever-so-slowly. She returned to the utility room to put away the floor sign but returned to the main floor to once more look around and make sure she was done for the night.

Tina saw her. "Time for the end of your shift?"

"I hope so," she said. "It's been a bit of a long day."

"Is this your only job?" Tina asked with a frown.

Hailee hesitated and then shrugged. "No, I have another job too."

Tina nodded. "I figured as much. It's probably not enough hours here, if you've got bills to pay."

Hailee's smile slipped. "Bills to pay, yes, that's one way to look at it." She turned away, and then she looked back at Tina and asked, "Will he be okay?"

"Who?" Tina asked, looking at her in surprise.

"The patient I called you for."

"I hope so," Tina said with a smile. "He's such a handsome man with his dark Moorish looks," she said. "You probably couldn't see for the lighting, but he's got dark hair, thick eyebrows, and an immaculately chiseled jaw."

Hailee nodded and hesitantly said, "He seemed like he was in a lot of pain."

"Well, he's doing better now," Tina said. "He has not

been too forthcoming about asking for help, and sometimes, well, sometimes you just don't know when people will need more care."

"I can understand that," Hailee said. She wasn't even sure why she was talking to Tina. It was so opposite to what Hailee usually did. But finally feeling a little awkward, she smiled and said, "Have a good evening."

"You too," Tina called out.

As Hailee grabbed her purse and readied to leave, she found herself taking the long way around and going past that same door. As she walked by, she whispered, "Good night. Sleep well."

In her mind, she wondered if he heard her but knew no way he could have, unless he had acute hearing. But, if he was lying in bed, waiting for morning to come, and could hear her footsteps, maybe he had heard her speak. Embarrassment burned through her, and she quickly rushed past. When she thought she heard his voice call out, she stopped and swore and then retraced her steps. At the door, she asked, "Are you okay?"

"Open the door, please," the voice commanded.

She hesitated and then turned the knob and pushed it open slightly. She stuck her head around the corner into the darkened room. "Hey," she said. "Can I do something for you?"

"I just wanted to say *thank you*," he said.

She straightened and stepped in slightly. "Why?"

"Because you called a nurse for me, and, if you hadn't done that, I'd be in a whole lot more pain right now."

She nodded and said, "You're welcome."

As she went to leave, he whispered, "Stop."

She hesitated again and looked toward him. But she

couldn't see him for shadows. "Do you need anything else?"

His voice was hesitant, almost like hers, when he said, "It's just nice to talk to somebody."

Her eyebrows shot up. "You're in a center full of people," she said. "Don't you visit with others?"

"Not really," he said. "I haven't been good about putting myself out there."

She could sympathize in an instant. "I'm not very good at it myself."

"I hear you every night," he said.

"Oh," she said. "I didn't realize I made so much noise. I'm sorry."

"No," he said. "You don't understand. It's a good noise."

She frowned. "How can it be a good noise?"

"It reminds me that I'm alive and that this is the real world. It tells me that I'm not still caught up in my nightmares. Yet sometimes I wonder if being in my nightmares is the only place that I'm comfortable anymore. But then I wake, and I hear your mop moving back and forth on the floor."

She could sense the surprise in his own voice, as if he was shocked he was talking to her. She understood the sentiment. "As long as it's not stopping you from sleeping," she said slowly.

"No, not at all. It's restful. It's …" He seemed to reach for a word and then stopped because he didn't know what he meant. "It's security," he whispered.

That just floored her. Because that was the last thing she'd expected. "The sound?" she asked. "The normalcy of it? The rhythm of it?"

"All of the above," he said. "It means I'm safe. It means I'm not still on the roadside, staring up at the sky, wondering what happened to my world."

Her heart softened. "I'm sorry. It seems like you've lived through some traumatic events. I just ... I can't imagine trying to put it behind you and moving on."

"And yet, that's what they tell us to do, as if it's so easy. It's not," he said, his voice deepening. "It seems impossible to let go and to move on."

"I understand," she whispered.

"Do you?" This time there was almost a detached sarcasm to his words, as if he'd heard that many times and thought that people were just plain pathetic.

"Not just the patients have been through rough times in their lives," she said with a little more strength to her tone than she expected. As if she didn't want him criticizing her, but, at the same time, she didn't want to explain either.

"You're right," he said in surprise. "And sometimes I need to be reminded of that."

"I'm sorry. I'm not trying to be insensitive," she whispered.

"No."

She could see his hand wave in the darkness.

"It's fine. I would much prefer people talk to me and treat me as a normal human being instead of somebody to be coddled and spoken softly to, in case I erupt."

"Is erupting something that you do?" she asked in surprise.

"I didn't think so, but it still seems as if everybody walks around me as if I'll explode at any moment."

"Interesting," she said. "Maybe they aren't anticipating an explosion as much as a cracking."

"WHAT'S INTERESTING ABOUT it?" he asked, wondering about her last words. "I would have said I was a fairly balanced personality. But since I've arrived here ..."

"I imagine nobody wants to cause you a setback or to do anything that would in any way slow your healing."

"And how would they know what would do that?" He was genuinely curious.

"I don't know," she said. "But, for me, it seemed like, as soon as disaster struck, everybody either sank out of sight and completely jumped ship or spoke as if I'd suddenly lost my hearing instead of my child."

A gasp came from the bed.

She frowned and winced. "I'm sorry. I didn't mean to say that."

"No," he said. "I appreciate the honesty. I'm surrounded by people in similar situations, trying to recover from their own hell. I know I can't be sympathetic to anyone else because I can't even be sympathetic to myself. I feel incredibly vulnerable here, and yet, at the same time, I have this sense that I don't deserve to be here."

"Wow," she said. "How is it you could possibly think you don't deserve to be here?"

"Two other people died," he said. "I should have been with them."

"I wanted to die too," she said, tears in her eyes and pain clogging her throat. "All I ever wanted was to be with my son."

"But our wants don't matter," he said. "Because, for whatever reason, we're forced to live with the losses of those who were with us."

"I know." Then, unable to handle anymore, she said, "I have to leave." And, with that, she closed the door and left.

Heath stared at the closed door for a long moment, hating that she'd left but realized that it had been a turning point for him regardless. He just didn't know in what way or how. He tucked himself under the blankets and pulled the pillow under his head to support his neck and then closed his eyes.

This time, he fell asleep with a smile on his face.

# Chapter 5

THIS WAS A pattern they set every night. Hailee worked her same routine, cleaning everything else before the floors, all the while waiting for the moment when she came to his room. Then slowly mopping the hallway floor outside his door. Something was almost spiritual about it. Yet she knew that anybody else would think she was a fool. It was such an odd feeling, yet almost one with a sense of honor to know he was listening to her—dare she say, *for her*? Her mopping sounds helped him feel grounded in this reality and kept him away from his nightmares. Who'd have thought it?

On the second evening in a row, he'd called out to her.

She'd stopped and spoken with him again. And then again on the third night. And a pattern had developed, and she didn't know if it was healthy or not, but it was an encounter she looked forward to now. This continued for seven nights in a row, and she was due to be off for the next two. She'd taken several more shifts to stay for these last two nights, and she'd slowly learned a little bit from the nurses about his condition.

She understood that he'd been driving a vehicle which blew up and that he blamed himself for the loss of his friends. Her grief and his held such similarities that she felt a kinship to him. Yet, at the same time, she knew that he wouldn't appreciate the sympathy.

He was so wrapped up in his guilt that he didn't know
he could turn and walk through a doorway and leave some of
that guilt behind. And how did she know that? Because she
hadn't been ready to see it either. She'd done everything she
thought she could do, but it hadn't been enough. So her
guilt had continued to destroy her. Her child hadn't been
meant to live in this world for very long, and the six months
that Jacob had been in her arms were the most blessed that
she'd ever experienced. But he'd been born with a severe
heart condition, and multiple surgeries had just made his life
one of pain and agony—and her own just as bad.

For any loving mother would have gladly borne all those
surgeries and all that pain and agony for the sake of her
child. A mother's greatest anguish is to watch her child
suffering from anything, whether physically or emotionally.

When five-months pregnant, she'd found out in her
doctor's checkup that there were problems with her pregnan-
cy, and her ob-gyn had suggested she let go of her unborn
child. But she couldn't do it, couldn't even begin to contemplate such a thing. He was her son. He lived and breathed
within her already, regardless if she had yet to give birth to
him. He deserved to have every breath he took and deserved
to fight for the next one.

But her husband hadn't agreed. They'd fought bitterly.
He'd turned and walked.

And the person she needed most at that moment had
abandoned her and their unborn child. That had been one of
many very long and very hard lessons for her from there on
out.

Her son had been gone from her life for one year now.
Twelve lonely months of trying to pay off medical bills so
large that everything she threw at them just bounced off the

total due, not even making a dent. She had no reprieve.

She wasn't even sure she could ever get clear of this massive debt. Her husband had divorced her, and she was free and clear of him, but he refused to pay any medical bills, citing that he had agreed with the doctor for her to have the recommended abortion. So it was her fault that she was suffocating under the mountain of bills—not his fault. The lawyers had been grim-faced over it all, and there'd been no happy resolution.

She'd gotten up and walked away from him and the attorneys and the paperwork that she had signed, knowing that it would be a long time before she could ever trust or believe in anybody like that again. But, at the same time, she had been bravely taking one step in front of the other. When she thought about Jacob now, she still fought tears but also wore a smile every second.

Hot tears burned the back of her eyes even now, but they weren't pouring down her cheeks. And what she did every day honored Jacob's presence in her life by honoring those debts she had to pay and honoring her commitments to relinquish her guilt, possibly to forgive her ex-husband at some future date. After that, maybe she'd finally take a step forward. She planned to never have another child. The pain and loss were too incredibly debilitating to go through again.

And, like these military men feeling survivor's guilt, all she could think about for the longest time was that it shouldn't have been Jacob who died. It should have been her …

Even though she hadn't done anything to contribute to Jacob's death, she'd brought him into this world, knowing he could have a hard and painful life.

It also felt like she hadn't done anything to add to his

life, and yet she'd been there as much as she could every day. Jacob never really made it out of the ICU. The hospital had done what they could to reduce the bills initially too. But still, some of them had to be paid. And she didn't have a support system or a network of family and friends to help pitch in, not monetarily, not emotionally, not physically.

It'd been all she could do to make a minimum payment. But she was doing what she needed to do, and that was working two jobs to keep some of the bills at bay. She paid a bunch of them down, but it would be a couple more years before she could even begin to see her way clear, and that's only if the hospital agreed to the latest proposal made by her attorney.

She had a friend who was a lawyer, and he'd submitted proposals that seemed like pennies on the dollar, so she could climb out of this hole. They were still waiting to see if the hospital would agree to this amount or would come back with a counteroffer, but even that reduced figure would be way more than she could get clear of anytime soon.

As she worked the mop back and forth along the hallway, she knew that he would be without her for the next two nights, and she worried that he would not get back to sleep if he woke up in the night. Could she tell the other cleaning lady to come and do this piece last? Or would that just seem so bizarre and cause an investigation into her relationship with a patient? A relationship based entirely on healing.

And yet, how could she begin to explain it? It was obscure. But the connection was there, a little bit at least. In fact, that connection and that sense of doing something for another human being was helping her too. How odd. So she didn't want to lose whatever it was, and she didn't want to slow down his healing. If her mopping the floor helped him return to sleep, then she was all for it, no matter how bizarre it may seem.

As for her looming hospital bills, she couldn't just spend her life comparing the numbers to see how far apart the hospital bills were from what she earned. The fact of the matter was, she was doing the best she could, and she would keep doing that. She would keep putting one foot in front of the other for as long as she could. Until she dropped from exhaustion. And, when she came to such a stopping point, if it wasn't enough, then it wasn't enough, and she'd find another way.

As she got to his door, she smiled as he called out. She stopped, placed her mop against the wall, walked to the door, then stuck her head around the corner, and said, "You should be sleeping."

"Can't sleep," he said. "Not until I hear your mop."

"On that note," she said, "I won't be here for the next two nights."

*SILENCE.*

"Why not?" he asked, dread in his heart. He really did not sleep well until she came past his room with her mop.

"It's my days off," she said apologetically. "I took an extra couple shifts, so I was here for the last two nights. But I do need a break."

"Of course you do," he said immediately, hating that he would lie here awake at night and wonder what she was doing. He didn't understand their connection but acknowledged that it existed. They shared … something. Some odd, twisted relationship between her mop, him, and his sleep.

He smiled bravely and said, "I hope you'll enjoy the next couple days."

"I'll be at another job," she said slowly. "So I don't think *enjoy* is quite the right word."

"You have two jobs?"

She hesitated, then nodded. "Medical bills."

"Right," he said softly. "Thankfully that is not a burden I have to bear."

She smiled and closed the door slowly behind her.

He laid there though, thinking about that pain of losing somebody and then still paying for the medical bills on top of it. What a horrible reminder. And given what she had said about her son, she had a mountain of debt to pay off. More years of remembering you were paying a bill that somebody had incurred while trying to save your child who couldn't be saved. Just the repetitive acknowledgment of that pain would be brutal.

He wished he could do something, but she was one of a million people he suspected with those kinds of medical bills, and how wrong was that? How do you ease that burden of so many? Or in what way could her burden be lifted? The last thing he had was money. Or not much. He was fine, his needs taken care of, but no pot of gold in the bank awaited him.

The government paid all his medical bills. He didn't know what he was supposed to do when he was back on his feet again. He would need retraining to make a living because he couldn't live off his benefits for long. He might find himself like her, cleaning floors to survive. Wouldn't that be a twist of fate? He should have enough to not have to do that, but she was doing honest work, and he could see how that honest work meant a lot, especially to her. Anything she could do to get back out from under her massive medical debts would be a huge boon.

He closed his eyes and thought about it, wondering if maybe he could help in some way.

# Chapter 6

Hailee made her way up the long ramp to the main floor of Hathaway House. She'd sent Dani an email early, asking if she could have a meeting with her. She was hopeful that her request would be granted, but she had yet to get up the nerve to even ask for it. But now she had been forced into making this change. As she walked into the front reception area, she recognized a new girl who had started a few days ago. "Hey, Caitlin. How are you doing?" she asked.

Caitlin looked up with a bright smile. "Hey, Hailee. How were your days off?"

Hailee shrugged and said, "It was fine." But of course it wasn't. She'd worked. That's all she ever did. But that wasn't for anybody else to worry about.

As she walked past, Dani called out, "Hailee, come on in."

She walked in and closed the door. "Hey, Dani. Sorry. I didn't mean to make this cloak-and-dagger-ish. I just wondered ..." She stopped.

Dani pointed at the two visitor chairs. "Hey, sit down. Relax. You're not due on for quite a few hours, aren't you?" She looked at her watch, frowned, and faced Hailee. "Or do you need to change your shift?"

"No, my shift is fine," she said, then hesitated.

"I can't help if you don't tell me what the problem is,"

Dani said gently, a sly smile on her face.

Hailee laughed. "You've already helped so much that it feels wrong to ask anything more of you."

"That's not the issue at all," Dani said. "All I've done is give you a job, and I'd give you a better one, if you'd let me."

"But I can't afford to let go of the one job," she said. "Yet it seems I might be forced to."

Dani frowned at that. "Well, if you tell me what you're making at both of them, maybe I can help."

At that, Hailee hesitated. This isn't what she had expected, and she didn't know what to say about that patient's need for Hailee's nighttime floor mopping, but then she hadn't been here for two nights anyway. Maybe he had managed without her. She sagged into the chair. "I was wondering if you had a staff room available," she said in a rush. As Dani's eyebrows shot up, Hailee took a deep breath and said, "I really need to cut back my expenses."

"Those damn bills, huh?"

"Yes," she said. "The lawyer still hasn't heard back on the latest proposal for the medical bills."

"*Hmm*," Dani said, frowning. "They should be lucky you're working as hard as you are, trying to pay them back."

"But it's so much money."

"Let me take a look at what I have available," Dani said.

"I know it's for your medical staff," Hailee rushed in to add.

"It doesn't matter who it's for," Dani said. "If I've got something that will help, then I'm all for it. Do you really think it'll help though?"

"It'll save me some back and forth traveling time for sure," Hailee said slowly. She'd been thinking about this a lot over these last several hours. "I don't know how much you charge your residents for the housing."

"I don't," Dani said. And then, with a clipped nod, she added, "That alone would help you, wouldn't it? Do you have much furniture to move?"

"I sold everything. I've been living in a tiny studio apartment in town."

"So how hard would it be to move you here?"

"Just loading up my car might take two runs." She tried to keep the anxious tone out of her voice, but it was hard because Dani could save Hailee quite a bit of money. Yet how was she supposed to ask for something like that? She wasn't very good at asking for help.

"You don't have much at home, so that'll make your move easier," Dani said, as she checked through the screens on her monitor. "You're right. We do have a lot of staff in residence here."

Hailee sat back and watched as Dani continued to click through her records. Hailee wondered if Dani even had any free spaces or if everything was full.

"And your employee numbers must move up and down all the time," Hailee said. "So, if you need to keep an empty apartment for incoming staff, then I understand totally."

Dani smiled at her. "If I had an accountant on staff, she could find this instantly." Dani tilted her head and raised her eyebrows at Hailee. "But I don't. And I can't even answer you about availability until I check through these records," she said. "So either grab a coffee and come sit back down and let me do this *or* disappear and let me do this."

At that, Hailee burst out laughing. "Got it," she said. "I'll go grab a coffee." She stopped at the doorway and looked back at Dani. "Do you want one?"

Dani looked up, smiled, and said, "I'd love one, thanks."

With that, Hailee headed toward the cafeteria. She was rarely here during the day and never midafternoon, but, since she'd finished at her bookkeeping job early, she was here now. She desperately wanted to stay here. Just a place where she could live and work and save a little bit more money so that she could get out of debt faster. A year here would help a lot. The lawyer had made it very clear that, if she made an attempt to pay the hospital bills, then there was a good chance that he could negotiate that bill down a good 50 percent—or even 75 percent. That would get her back on her feet in the foreseeable future, while she was still capable of working. Indeed, it would make a huge difference, and she could probably get most of it paid off within several years. But, without this write off, she might as well declare bankruptcy right now, and that was a very depressing concept. Did that even clear medical bills?

In the cafeteria, she was surprised to see a number of people, from patients to staff. Some were sitting together, and some were sitting alone. Lots of meetings seem to be happening. From what she saw, some of the therapists were off in a huddle to one side. As she walked down the aisle, she accidentally went in along the foodservice line.

Dennis popped up and said, "Can I get you something?"

She shook her head. "I'm not starting my shift yet. I just came to get coffee for Dani and me."

He stopped, frowning at her, and asked, "Are you paying for food elsewhere?"

She looked at him in surprise. "Of course I am!"

His frown deepened.

She smiled and said, "Remember? I don't live here."

"*Hmm.*"

She could see it bothered him. "Don't worry about it,"

she said carelessly. She walked over to the coffee area and poured two cups. She didn't even remember how Dani liked hers. She turned to see Dennis still staring at her. "Do you know how Dani takes her coffee?"

He chuckled and said, "A little bit of cream."

She smiled, added a splash of cream, picked up the two mugs, and said, "Thanks." As she headed out, she continued to feel Dennis's eyes boring into her back. She hadn't even considered that extra cost. And now she worried if she'd asked Dani for way too much. She had already given Hailee a job. But to expect Dani to cover Hailee's housing costs was too much because Hailee hadn't taken into account her food costs here too.

Although she didn't eat much, it was still an extra expense. And she hadn't even looked at her own budget to see how much it would have saved her because she wasn't eating well now because she didn't dare. She shook her head. As she walked in, she announced, "Forget about it."

Dani looked up at her in surprise, saw the coffee, and smiled. "Thanks. What do you mean, *forget about it?*"

"I wasn't thinking," she said. "But, for me to live here, I'd also be eating here, and that would be an added cost on you."

Dani chuckled. "Are you serious?"

Hailee sat down, frowning. "Of course I'm serious," she said. "I don't want anything to impact your ability to run this place."

"The food is good and all," Dani said, "but one more mouth really doesn't make a whole lot of difference in the overall scheme. In case you hadn't noticed, we offer a ton of food all the time." Then she stopped and looked at her. "But, of course, you don't know that, do you? And you probably don't even eat here, do you?"

Hailee shook her head. "No. I was just talking to Dennis, and he basically hopped up to ask me what I wanted to eat."

"That's Dennis," Dani said. "One of the most willing staff members we have here."

"He didn't sound pleased that I didn't eat here," Hailee said with a frown, still feeling bad at her oversight. "Does everybody eat here?"

"If you work here, you're welcome to eat here," Dani said. "It's one of the perks. We do have a lot of extra people, and yet there are leftovers all the time."

If Hailee could even get some of the leftovers, that would save her even more with her food bill. She shook her head. "You've already done so much for me."

Dani sighed. "I want you to tell me point-blank how much money you make at the other job."

Hailee hesitated.

"Okay, let's go by ranges," she said. "Do you make over forty?"

"Hell no," Hailee said. "I don't. Why?"

"Adding in your earnings from this job, do the two of them pay you fifty?"

Hailee had to stop and think about it, and then she slowly shook her head. "Close maybe, but no."

"So then, how about you come in as my accountant? Which is what I've been trying to get you to do for months. I'll pay you what I paid my last one, which was fifty-eight a year to start, and we can move up from there later. Plus I have a room for you. It's actually scheduled for my accountant," she said with a smile. "And, yes, that's my added bonus to entice you to take this job. And, of course, all your meals would be free here. So basically you would have fifty-eight grand minus taxes at the end of the day."

Hailee stared at her, her jaw dropping. "Seriously?"

"Absolutely," Dani said with a nod. "I should be paying more than that for the accountant. That's something you can help me figure out when you're in the position. We'll do some shifts in the bookkeeping work, so that I can see where all the costs are coming from. I have it here in front of me, but, at the same time, I'm sure I could do some better record-keeping."

"Are you positive you need an accountant?" she asked. "You handle all the books."

"I do," Dani said, "and it takes me forever."

"So do you need an accountant part-time?" Hailee countered.

"No, I need a full-time accountant." Dani laughed, and the sound was joyous and bright, putting a smile on Hailee's face.

"I get that you care, but I don't want you being overly concerned about me," Hailee said.

Dani shook her head. "If you come on board as my accountant, we both get the benefit of that."

Hailee looked at her, smiled gently, and, with a deep *whoosh*, said, "Thank you. I accept."

"Good," Dani said, her smile widening, lighting up her face. "Now, how long before you can start?"

"Well, I got notice from my landlord that my rent is going up next month, plus layoffs will happen soon at my day job, which is why I was asking about a place to live," Hailee said with an unhappy frown. "My boss in town is already asking for people to step up and quit, to avoid forcing others into a layoff. If I do quit, I'm not supposed to go back anymore. And this month's rent is due as it is, so I already talked to my landlord about maybe being late this month."

"In that case, we'll send somebody back with you, and you'll get moved in today," Dani said. "Okay?"

Hailee shook her head, amazed and stunned at how fast everything had just shifted. "Are you sure?"

"Hell, yes, I'm sure," Dani said. "On the downside, I might have to hire somebody to replace you for cleaning. People have noticed what a great job you've been doing."

"Well, if you don't need a full-time accountant, is it possible that I could still do some of the cleanings?"

"No, that won't work."

"It'll work if we say it works," Hailee said stubbornly and hoped she hid the tiny note of desperation in her voice. She had an ulterior motive for continuing the cleaning, but that was a completely different topic.

HEATH TOSSED AND turned on his bed. He'd come back in from physio exhausted, but nothing was helping him sleep. Since his cleaning lady wasn't here, he couldn't wake up and hear the same rhythmic motion that immediately put him back to sleep again. He knew it was stupid. It was one of those little things that he didn't dare tell anybody about because it made no sense.

Not only that it made no sense but it also made him sound like he was off his rocker, and he *really* couldn't afford more of that. He already knew that everything he said and did was analyzed and then ripped apart to look for hidden meanings and nuances as to why he was struggling so much.

He'd told his medical team that he was having night-mares, and they'd offered all kinds of suggestions to help relieve some of the stress, but nothing would ease his guilt. He understood survivor's guilt was a real thing, and so did they, but, so far, nothing they had suggested was helping. And he wanted it to, but, at the same time, he hadn't told them the entire story. He kept it locked in the back of his mind. He was too ashamed to tell anyone. He didn't think it was essential to share; it was something he had to work through himself. But now, after two days without decent sleep, nothing was going right. He was short-tempered and angry, and all his interactions caused him more and more stress.

On that note, a hard knock came at his door. He groaned. "I'm sleeping," he growled.

The door opened instead. Heath glared at his intruder. Shane stood there with his hands on his hips and glared right back.

"What do you want?" Heath muttered. He shifted, hating the wince that crossed his face at the pain rippling up and down his body. But Shane immediately moved to Heath's side and, using competent hands, shifted Heath's body until he lay flat on his stomach. Shane pulled the pillow out from under Heath's head and said, "Just lie there for a moment."

It was all Heath could do to not immediately retort back with something much harsher. Then Shane got to work on Heath's neck. When he felt a moment later the tension release, Heath whispered, "Thank you."

"Is this why you're having such a crappy day?" Shane asked, as he worked up and down Heath's spine.

Heath knew that Shane could feel the knots and the agony from the torn muscles as they had healed but left scar tissue that tightened so badly they wouldn't stretch. It was all Heath could do to stop the tears from coming into his eyes. He turned his head so his face was pressed against the sheet, holding back as much as he could.

Shane suddenly stopped and said, "No point in me releasing the knots in your back if you continue to hold it all within your head and your heart. I've seen bigger and harder and tougher men cry. You have to let this go."

Heath couldn't stop the shake of his head and the instinctive tightening of his back.

Immediately Shane grabbed Heath's trapezius gently and squeezed ever-so-lightly. "These? These shoulder muscles are sending the rest of your chest muscles off-balance," he said. "And this tension is from you resisting. You need to calm it down." He shifted Heath a little bit lower in the bed and then resumed work. His hands were coated in something. He massaged lightly and then not-so-lightly, as he continued to work layer after layer at the insertion points on each and every muscle on his back.

When Heath realized he no longer shook with the pain but was actually shaking with relief, he didn't know what to say. The tears had stopped flowing, and finally he could lay his head to the side and take a deep, normal breath.

"And after that deep breath," Shane ordered, "take another one. I want you to think of your chest now." As he said this, Shane placed his hands on either side of Heath's rib cage. "Think of your chest as a box. I want you to imagine your shoulders and arms as the sides of the box. ... And I want your head ..." He placed his hand on the top of Heath's head. "To act as the knob on the lid of this box. When you breathe, try to push out all four walls of the box, then lift the lid, meaning stretching your head up. I want you to maximize that image with each breath and then slowly release it."

With that visual, Heath had no problem following Shane's instructions. After three deep breaths, he could already feel some of his tension easing.

"If you were standing right now," Shane said, "and in front of a mirror, where you could actually see your body working, you would note your body starting to straighten up and to align properly, using that box method. And when you do get up, I want you to practice that box exercise three times and widen that box as much as you can by filling your lungs, then lifting the lid off that box as high as it will go. Can you do that?"

"I can do that," Heath said. "My chest is feeling a lot better."

"Yes, it is," he said. "You're missing half a rib, and your muscles have to compensate for it," he said. "But, when you end up so strained all the time, they can't even begin to work because they're trying to pull against that tension you hold there. Then what happens is all your back muscles seize up, trying to do the job that the front muscles are supposed to be doing."

"What you're saying is, I need to relax more." A note of bitterness was in his tone. "I can't even sleep right now," Heath whispered.

"If you can't find ways to sleep on your own, the drugs do help."

"They give me terrible nightmares," he muttered.

Shane's hand stopped for a brief moment on his back. "Interesting," he said.

"What's interesting about it?"

"Sometimes drugs get in under your subconscious and work things to the surface. I'm not much for chemical inducements, but sometimes it's needed to get your body to rest. Muscle relaxants would also help, but I understand that you're struggling with a reaction to those."

"Yes," he said. "I'm getting terrible water retention from them." He lifted his ankle, since there was only one left to show Shane.

Shane immediately said, "Okay, I'll get down there in a minute." By the time he had worked all the way down, massaging Heath's massive quads and thighs down to his calves, Shane gently stroked a couple places and then pressed down, Heath almost screamed at the unexpected pain.

"I gather that's painful," Shane said in a half-joking manner. "We'll work on that area next."

And he kept working, easing and smoothing out some of the tension and the swelling in the ankle. "This is a lot of the reason why you're getting some of this water retention." And finally, after at least fifteen minutes of massaging that leg, Shane shifted and said, "I'll leave it alone now. It's had enough." And he reached over and placed his hand on Heath's knee and what was left of his other leg. "Now, how is this one?"

"It's fine," Heath muttered. But he was already tense and afraid that Shane would start working on it.

"And yet it's apparently not," Shane said with a note of humor in his voice.

"Every time you touch me, it hurts."

"But does it still hurt?"

"Not the other parts, no, but I know the process of getting there is painful."

"It can be, yes," he said. "Let's get you into the wheelchair."

"And if I don't want to?"

"Well, you can resist all you want, but it'll just hold you back. So why would you not go into the wheelchair?"

"It depends on where you are taking me," he said.

At that, Shane laughed. "I would suggest the hot tub."

Immediately Heath shifted so he was sitting, and he stared at Shane with a doubtful look. "Are you joshing me?"

"No," he said. "I'm not. But it occurred to me that that's one of the things we should be working on. You can also do exercises in the hot tub."

"Is that all you think about? Exercises?"

Shane chuckled. "No, maybe not. But you, dear sir, need to get your body back into alignment. And it's not doing that on its own." He pulled up the wheelchair and set it beside the bed. "Get in."

"Are these shorts okay?"

Shane nodded. "Yep, those are fine. Let's grab a towel and get you down there." He tossed the towel over the back of the wheelchair and pushed Heath out the door.

"Am I supposed to be powering my own wheelchair?"

"Nope, not right now," Shane said. "I don't want you messing up the work I just did."

"And pushing my own wheelchair would mess it up?"

"Depends on your technique," he said. "The mood and the tension that you're under right now could very well do that."

At that, Heath subsided. He couldn't believe he was going to the hot tub. His body was craving something, and he hoped the hot water would work for his muscles. He needed sleep, and he needed it in a big way.

# Chapter 7

A S SOON AS she walked out of Dani's office, Hailee felt
a whole lot better. But then Dani called out, "Hey!"

Hailee stepped back in again. "Hey what?"

"I've got Robert on-site with one of the trucks that we
use for deliveries in town," she said. "He's free. I want you to
get in your car, take him to your place, pack up, and try to
move in here tonight, if you can."

Hailee looked at her in surprise.

"You can't stay where you are. Go ahead and quit your
town job. No point in you going back and forth," Dani said.
"And you can start work tomorrow morning, if you're up to
it. Otherwise we can hold off another day."

"I really have nothing much to pack up, and, although it
probably won't all fit in my car, I don't need a big truck."

"Well, we have a pickup. Would that be better?"

At that, Hailee smiled. "That would be perfect." While
she stood here, talking to Dani, a grizzled old man walked
toward them. There was a spring to his step, and he dangled
keys in his fingers. He poked his head in Dani's office and
asked, "What's up?"

"We're moving Hailee here to one of the residences," she
said. "She doesn't have much and figures it's too much for
the big truck but maybe one of the pickups. Can you go with
her and give her a hand?"

"Sure," he said. He looked over at Hailee. "You'll finally join the funny farm, will you?"

"Well, I've already been here for a while," Hailee said with a big smile. "Now I guess I'm moving in full-time."

"It's the best place to be. Now come on. Let's go. I got to meet the missus coming in to pick me up later. She wants me to do some drapery shopping or some such thing," he said with a big eye roll.

Hailee laughed. "Do you have the time? Otherwise I don't want to take you away from your wife's appointment."

"It's twenty minutes to town. I don't think you got much stuff, if Dani says you don't," he said. "If nothing else, I can meet you, drop you off, go meet the wife, then come back to pick you up."

"That might not be a bad idea," Hailee said. She hadn't been looking forward to packing up what little she had in front of him.

"Good enough," Dani said, waving her fingers. "Now get lost so I can get some work done." But there was a laugh in her voice and a smile on her face.

On their way to the parking lot, Hailee called her boss in town to quit her day job, so somebody else didn't lose theirs. She'd talk to her landlord in person soon. When she hung up, she was at her car and gave Robert her address. "I'm probably a slower driver than you."

"Yeah, you probably are. Follow me into town. I'll get you there in no time." He winked at her, making her chuckle. He walked over to one of the pickups parked off to the side, hopped in, turned it on, and pulled out. He waited for her to get in her car, turn over the engine, and come in behind him.

And that's how they drove back into town. He did drive

faster than she usually did, but it didn't seem like a dangerous pace. They made it to her apartment in no time, leaving
her feeling incredibly upbeat. Then he parked outside and
said, "Show me your place, so I have an idea of what kind of
work we got before us."

She nodded and led him to her second-story studio.

He looked around at the small space, shook his head,
and said, "Wow, not much here."

"And it's not my bed or my couch," she said. He looked
at her in surprise, and she shrugged. "It's been a rough
couple years. I had to sell everything to pay medical bills,"
she said quietly.

Instantly understanding flashed on his face. "Those out-
rageous medical bills could kill anybody," he muttered.
"How long do you think you need to pack?"

She shook her head. "An hour or two maybe?"

"Do you have any boxes?"

"No," she said, looking around. "I've got a few pieces of
luggage that I'll take my clothing in, but I don't have
anything for my kitchen stuff. I can use garbage bags for the
bathroom stuff and linens."

"I'll get some boxes," he said. "You start pulling out stuff
to pack. We should be done with this in a couple hours, if
not half of that." Without another word, he disappeared.

She couldn't even begin to process how quickly her life
had flipped around, but she pulled out her suitcases, opened
them up, and dumped in her clothing and personal stuff. She
didn't even worry about how well she packed. It was more
important to just have it done, so she could move out. As
soon as she had the suitcases full, she grabbed a couple big
black garbage bags that she had and stuck in her comforter,
blankets, and bedding. She could do laundry at Dani's. With

that done, she headed to the bathroom, and, in smaller garbage bags, she quickly loaded everything of hers here, wrapping up breakables in towels.

By the time Robert came back with a few boxes, she was mostly done.

Robert looked at her in approval. "Not too shabby. You're not worried about getting it all neat and tidy, are you?"

"It seemed more important," she said with a laugh, "to just get it done."

"Exactly," he said. "And you don't have very much here anyway." He went to the kitchen and pulled out a few dishes, then looked at her and asked, "Is this all yours?"

"The dishes and the cutlery are the landlady's. The coffeemaker is mine. The teakettle is mine. The food in the fridge is mine, and the food in the cupboards is mine," she said. With four boxes folded into shape and a fifth one now ready, they quickly unloaded the cupboards. Robert folded together two more boxes for her to pack up the fridge. Then they hauled everything out, and, before long, she stared at one last box that was half empty.

While she walked through the small space, cleaning cloth in hand, confirming she had everything of hers out, the landlady walked in, took a look, and said, "Oh, good. I have somebody interested in this room now. In which case I can let you off this month's rent."

"It's perfect timing for me too," Hailee said, "as I'm almost done cleaning up." She'd already done the bathroom and the kitchen area. "I'm just figuring out if I missed anything."

Together they went through every corner and looked under the bed. Then the landlady handed over her inspection report to Hailee, as she returned her key to the landlord, all while Robert was here to collect the last box. When Hailee stepped out and shut the door behind her, she stood for a moment, feeling a massive shift in her world. Then she ran down the stairs, feeling better today than she'd felt in a long time.

Robert waited for her at the truck. "Do we have everything now?"

She nodded. "I wonder if I could have gotten this all in the car."

"Not without two trips," he said. "Much easier to do it this way," he said. "And we'll get back in time," he said. "I'll still make the wife's appointment."

She laughed and said, "I'm following you. Let's go." And she got in her car and returned to Hathaway House. As she crossed the gates into the massive property, she could feel something inside ease further. If nothing else, she could give back to the world here. Surely somebody could use what she had to offer. As long as the lawyer kept fighting for a reduction in her medical bills, maybe she would see a light at the end of that tunnel someday too.

Robert pulled out in front of one of the buildings on the far side as Hailee parked beside him. They stood together on the sidewalk, and he motioned to one of the doors. She was surprised that she had already been assigned a room. She followed him and asked, "Do you know where I'm staying?"

"Yep. This is the hallway." And he opened it up, and she could see doors on either side leading down. "Each of these opens to their own private patio on one side, and we've got housing for thirty here. You're number four." As he said that, he opened up number four and let her in. It was twice the size of where she'd just come from, and a small loft held a bed. She looked up there and smiled. "Beds are here too?"

"Dani gave you one of the first ones," he said, as he headed back to the truck to grab the first of the boxes.

She raced behind him, laughing with joy. "I'll love being here," she cried out.

"It's a good place to be," he said. "Dani is a good woman."

"She has been a lifesaver for me," Hailee said.

Robert nodded. "She has a habit of picking up people who need help and giving them what they need so they can fly solo again."

"Well, that's an apt description. I hadn't really considered myself in that light, but that's the way it is."

"I didn't mean no insult," he said. "She's just known for helping out people."

As Hailee looked out at the paddock nearby, she could see several horses, a filly, and what looked like a little llama too. She stopped for a moment. "I don't even remember seeing these animals here."

"Well, that big black one is Dani's own personal horse, and the little llama is named Lovely. That partner right beside Lovely, that pretty multicolored horse there, spent all its time with the llama. And the other horses are strays or spares or whoever knows. Dani fosters and adopts anybody who needs a home."

For a long moment, Hailee stood here, realizing that she had just become one of Dani's fosters. It was an uncomfortable feeling. Especially for someone like Hailee, who hated to ask for help. Yet, when forced to ask, she really needed any help she could get. But, at the same time, she also knew that Dani had given Hailee a gift. A chance to get back on her feet and to find her way again.

Robert walked past her with another armload. "Come on, come on, come on," he said. "Otherwise you're explaining to the wife why I'm late."

She shouted out a bark of laughter and raced to his truck, grabbing the garbage bags. With one over her shoulder and the other one in her arms, she returned to her little apartment. Then did it again and again. And finally they were done.

Robert walked back outside and said, "Welcome to Hathaway House. You'll love it here." Then he hopped in his truck and drove away.

Hailee stood at the open hallway door and realized that it was never locked, so everyone could come in the same way. She went to her new apartment, typed in the code Robert gave her, and it unlocked in front of her. Then she stepped inside, walked outside through the double glass doors to her patio, and, from where she stood, she could see the paddocks and some of the horses from her apartment. She turned around in a big circle with her arms wide and laughed. "Thank you! Thank you! Thank you, Dani!"

Then she went inside to unpack and to get her house to rights before she returned to the main building. She knew she was supposed to go to work in the morning. But part of her desperately wanted to see how Heath was doing. She just didn't understand if that was something she was even allowed to do. Maybe she'd sneak by his room at two in the morning. But first things first. She needed to get settled in. Then everything else could come later.

HEATH SAT IN his wheelchair near the hot tub the next day,

once again persuaded by Shane to make his way down here. Heath wasn't quite as stiff and sore as he had been the previous day. Yesterday he'd had a hard time enjoying the heated water because it had soaked into his aching muscles and then zapped the strength away from him, the weather itself having taken what little bit he had left.

As Shane helped him out of the wheelchair and into the water, he said, "It shouldn't be too bad today."

"Well, it's better," Heath acknowledged, as he shifted in the water, almost groaning as the heat soaked into his body again. "I don't understand how it can feel so good, yet, at the same time, it exhausts me."

"It's the heat soaking into your muscles," Shane said, as he stepped down ever-so-slightly into the hot tub. He started working on Heath's shoulder. His rotator cuff had been badly damaged in the blast, while muscles holding the atlas bone underneath his skull had been weakened. Heath often got headaches when he sat up too much. "I want you to sit on this lower level over here."

Heath discovered the different levels to the hot tub. Shuffling slowly, he sat down on the lowest seat, feeling the warm water rise under his chin, soaking into the back of his neck. He rested his head along the wall to the hot tub and just groaned in relief.

"Now I don't want you to stay here too long," Shane warned. "Five minutes and then shift out."

"You mean, *fifty* minutes and then shift out," Heath said with a smile.

"Well, that's the first smile I've seen out of you in days," Shane said, "so we'll make it ten."

"If you get a laugh, can we make it twenty-five?"

"Nope, no more deals," Shane said. "I'll be right here.

I'll grab you another towel too. We didn't bring one from your room today."

"That's because we came straight from PT," he said. "You didn't let me get to my room."

"Nope," Shane said. "And I'll also bring over Jeff. He's one of our newer specialists on staff, and he'll work with you while you're in the water."

"Crap," Heath said, opening his eyes to glare up at Shane. "When am I off duty?"

"When were you off duty when you were in the navy?"

"Basically never," he said.

"And now you're recovering from your injuries until you're 100 percent, so the answer is basically *never* here too."

Heath hated to hear it, but he also understood the reasoning behind it. He just wished there was some get up and go that could be pumped into his system, so he didn't feel like everything was a waste of time, energy, and effort, because well, … at the core, of course, he didn't feel like he deserved any of it.

When he opened his eyes the next time, he felt an inner sense of being watched. He saw a young man, olive-skinned and heavily muscled, standing and staring at him, his hands on his hips.

"You *better* be Jeff," he said.

"Oh, I'm Jeff, but you sagged into that spot on the hot tub as if your bones and your muscles won't hold you up anymore."

"They won't," Heath acknowledged. And, true to form, he just let his body float up until the water churned around him, and he floated on top of the bubbles.

"Interesting," Jeff said, as he walked around the large hot tub, studying Heath's body.

"Interesting in what way?"

"Even floating, you're favoring your full-leg side."

"Well, doesn't that make sense? There's less of me to float on the right side," he said. "So I'm floating higher there because less weight's pulling me down."

At that, Jeff laughed. "Nope, that's not it at all. But you're still pulling away from your injured side."

"I would think that's normal."

"Some people pull away, and some people roll toward it," Jeff said. "Some people are more protective of that side, whereas other people still refuse to acknowledge that the injured part exists."

At that, Heath's eyes flew open, and he stared up at the bright sky above him. "Well, that sucks."

"Why is that?"

"Because that's me," he said. "I'm still pretending it doesn't exist. And, if I don't acknowledge it, maybe I don't have to actually live with it."

"Maybe," Jeff said, as he squatted down, still studying Heath but from his foot position. "It won't work long-term though."

"Well, apparently it didn't work short-term either," Heath said in disgust. "Don't you guys let us have any illusions?"

"No," Jeff said. "I used to run PT in the military." He shrugged. "Not a whole lot I haven't seen before."

"You don't look old enough to even have made the grade to get in," Heath said in disgust.

"That's because I'm healthy," Jeff said with a surprising answer. "I haven't been through a major trauma like you have. So the lines, the worry, and the stress aren't etched into my skin yet. I've lived, but it's been relatively easy so far."

"For that, I hate you," Heath said, his tone quiet and barely audible above the bubbles.

"No, you don't," Jeff said. "You'd like to be me, but you also know that your time is past."

"Yeah," Heath said. "A long time ago."

"But that doesn't mean," Jeff continued, "that you can't still be a whole lot better than you are."

"It doesn't feel like it," Heath said. "It feels more like I'm heading into the backside of sixty."

"If you don't get fixed up soon," he said, "you'll hit a body age of sixty very quickly. In the meantime, we can do a lot to keep your body improving to the point of being in its thirties again."

"Meaning, I'm already forty or fifty, per my body?"

"Yes, unfortunately," Jeff said bluntly, not pulling any punches. "Just like with any physical trauma, it ages your body. But it's the mental decline and that emotional stress which ages the rest of you so much faster."

Heath groaned. "So what do I have to do?"

"Get started, Heath. We have a lot to work on."

# Chapter 8

THE NEXT FEW days followed a simple pattern. Hailee would get up, shower, and then head to the cafeteria to grab a coffee, presenting herself at Dani's office by eight. The first morning, Dani was there on time to show Hailee where her new office would be, as well as her new computer and their filing system. As Dani walked out, she said, "Get yourself familiar. We'll have a ton of work soon enough, and I won't always be here at the same time. I'll start horseback riding in the mornings again, as much as I can."

"That sounds wonderful," Hailee said. "You should take more time off."

Dani tossed her a bright smile. "That's why I hired you."

Hailee just rolled her eyes at that. "Glad to hear it," she said.

"I do have a bunch of employee benefits materials and reimbursement stuff for you," Dani said. "We'll get to that in a bit. I've got a meeting here at nine. A phone conference." A secretive smile split her face as she headed back to her office. But then Dani was involved in a lot of different things. Not to mention trying to jump up funding for the several beds that she kept open for people who didn't have money.

It was one of the reasons Hailee really appreciated her friend's life philosophy about making sure that everyone helped others in need. No one person could help everyone because bills still had to be paid, but it was essential to help *someone* when you could. Like Dani was doing for Hailee.

But Hailee fully intended to give Dani excellent value. If Hailee hadn't lost her first accounting job, right after Jacob was born, she'd still be working at that same place, where she'd already worked for seven years. When they realized she was draining their medical benefits, she'd been laid off in a very suspicious manner. She couldn't seem to fight that because, according to them, all of a sudden, they'd lost several big clients and needed one less accountant.

She understood why they'd done it from a strictly numbers perspective, but it had been heartbreaking for her, along with too many more heartbreaks at the same time. And so disloyal to a long-term employee like her. It was highly illegal too, but, when Hailee's lawyer said that he could only do so much pro bono work for her and asked her if she wanted to go after her employer or try to get the medical debt reduced, she'd immediately gone for the reduction in her medical debt.

She sent him a quick email, telling him that she now had one full-time job at Hathaway House and gave him a new work email address where he could contact her. He sent a quick response, telling her that he was really happy for her and that he expected to have some news here within a week or so. She smiled and typed, *I hope so. I've lost weight because I can't afford to eat.*

She added a happy face because, now that she was here at Hathaway House, she *could* eat. Speaking of which, she hadn't had food yet. She frowned at that and wondered just what the deal was. She didn't want to take any food from Dani if it wasn't allowed and neither did she want to abuse the eight-to-four work system by eating on the job.

When the new girl at the front, Caitlin, hopped up and came around the corner, she stopped when she saw who was behind the desk in Hailee's new office. Caitlin smiled and said, "Wow, that's perfect," she said. "From cleaning lady to an accountant."

"Well, technically I was a cleaning lady *and* a bookkeeper, working two jobs to replace my original accountant's job, now back to being just an accountant," Hailee said with a chuckle. "I'm not proud. Workers work."

"But a very different paycheck," Caitlin said with an eyebrow raised.

"Absolutely," she said. But she didn't offer any information to clarify how she'd gone from the highs to the lows and back to the highs again.

Caitlin motioned down the hallway. "I'm getting coffee. Do you want one?"

Hailee smiled and hopped up. "Maybe. I'll come with you. I'm not exactly sure how the system here works."

"Oh, that's easy enough," Caitlin said, as she filled her in. "For lunch, we try to give way to all the patients. We have more time available to us to get there because we can come and go as we need to. The breakfast bar opens at six in the morning, but I've never really made it that early, so don't hold me to that. Maybe ask Dennis. And then dinner is between five and seven, I believe. I don't eat breakfast, but I'll often pick up a muffin and take it back to my desk."

"I wondered if we're allowed to eat on the job," Hailee confessed. "At my old job, I was allowed a cup of coffee but no food because of the possibility to drop crumbs into the keyboards."

"I think everybody here would starve then," Caitlin said

with a laugh. "But you're right, that was like my last job too. Dani doesn't mind, and her only restrictions on the food are, *if you take it, please eat it.* Because they don't want to waste any food. Here, the kitchen is very good at using up leftovers, and that has gone a long way to keeping her food costs down. Plus I see a lot of the staff willingly eating the leftovers for their meals."

"Makes sense to me," Hailee said. "I'm happy with leftovers too." She walked into the cafeteria to see Dennis with a big smile on his face.

"There you are. I've seen you in the evening, in the afternoon, and now in the morning."

"And you'll see me a little more often now," she said. "I'm working as the new accountant."

"Perfect," he said with a beaming smile. "I didn't see you here for breakfast though."

"I wasn't exactly sure what the protocol was."

"*If you work here, you eat here,*" Dennis said with a fat smile. "That doesn't mean necessarily I won't give you leftovers …"

She chuckled. "I'm pretty sure your leftovers are way better than no leftovers."

He chuckled, and she headed straight for the coffee, but he frowned at her. "Too much caffeine on an empty stomach is not good."

"Maybe not," she said, "but I just started. I don't really want to ruin my job already."

At that, Dani came up behind Hailee and said, "I should have gone over that with you anyway. I'm glad Dennis just said something. I often come in and do some work, and then I'll take a break and have breakfast. Put in the hours, get the job done, and I won't bother you about when you work and where you eat."

At that, Dennis handed over a beautiful omelet to Dani.

Hailee smiled and said, "Now this looks great."

Dani snagged an orange juice and some cutlery, and, with a wave to everyone, headed back to her office.

Caitlin said, "See? That's what I mean."

Hailee looked back at Dennis. He lifted up a second omelet and said, "One of the guys ordered it and then decided he didn't want it," he said coaxingly.

"But what's in it?" Hailee asked, eyeing the omelet.

"Steak and mushrooms," he said. She stared at him in surprise. He nodded, walked over, added a few hash browns and a couple fresh orange slices, then gave it to her. "Now eat up. You can't do the job if you have brain fog."

She chuckled. "Does that argument work for you?"

"Well, you're holding the omelet right now," he said, "so I guess so." He chuckled and headed into the kitchen, then turned and said, "Lunchtime starts at eleven and finishes at two. If you come a little later sometimes, it's better because it can get really crowded in here. Otherwise aim maybe for early."

"In other words, if it's busy, just come back?"

"Patients come first," he said, "but the staff is a very close second. Dani would tell you that she can't help the patients if she doesn't have a pleasant staff."

"I understand that philosophy," Hailee said with a big smile. "Besides, Dani is a sweetheart."

"She is," Dennis said. "And, because of her, this place does very well."

"Good to know." Carrying her omelet and coffee, she followed Caitlin back to the office area. As Hailee walked behind the receptionist, she asked, "Does anybody worry about getting fat here?"

"Well, I haven't worried about it," Caitlin said. "But, if I stay here much longer, I might have to." She held up the cinnamon bun she was taking back to her desk. "At least your meal is nutritionally sound. Mine's food for the soul. Yours is food for the body."

"Well, if my body wasn't so starved," Hailee said, "I'd have gone for soul food too."

And they both chuckled and headed to their respective desks.

SEVERAL DAYS LATER Heath sat in the outdoor dining section on the deck, letting the sunshine bathe his face. He was still gathering the energy to go back inside and get food. He'd gotten his coffee, and he was working on a second cup when Dennis had come around with the pot. Otherwise, Heath wouldn't have that still. The heavy massage sessions with Shane and the heavy workouts in the hot tub with Jeff had slowly built up some of Heath's muscles, but the pain and exhaustion had really whacked him out. He still wasn't sleeping at night. In fact, it was getting worse.

As he sat here, he thought he heard a familiar voice—*the cleaning lady.* He turned his head and listened intently to make sure. He twisted ever-so-slightly, mindful of his back and his neck, turning to see if he could put a body with the voice. He noticed one of the women from the front offices and another superslim, almost too slim, woman with dark hair and curls down over her shoulders, wearing a simple pair of white capris and a flowery blouse. She held a plate of food, and she had a big smile on her face.

He studied her for a long moment, but he couldn't hear her voice anymore. Disappointed and frustrated, he shifted back, staring outside past the deck. His cleaning lady was supposed to take two days off but hadn't come back in like a week now. And since then, he hadn't had a decent night's sleep. Something was magical about whatever they'd had before, and he needed that back.

Yet he could hardly ask some stranger to come and mop the floors at nighttime for him to sleep. Talk about a dependency issue that made no sense. As he sat here, wondering if he would make it to the cafeteria line or not, Dennis walked over and placed in front of Heath a platter of fried potatoes and eggs with ham and sausages. Heath looked at it, then up at Dennis in surprise.

"Saved you a trip," Dennis said. And he disappeared.

That was one of the things about Dennis. He saw things that other people didn't recognize, and he acted without other people needing to say anything. Heath didn't know if that was a good thing or not, but, as far as he was concerned, Dennis was solid gold. Somebody who saw a need and handled it without being told was an exceptional individual.

Heath dug into his breakfast with gusto. He may not have chosen quite the exact same things, but it didn't matter because it was fresh and hot, and it was in front of him. By the time he pushed away his empty plate, he was more than happy that he'd chosen to just sit and relax. Sometimes you had to stop and smell the roses instead of rush, rush, rush.

And it would have been a rush to get in before the long lines started, and then he would have felt self-conscious for stumbling forward on his crutches in front of a big crowd. He was getting a prosthetic foot for his right leg, and he knew he'd have to learn to walk all over again with it, but he was up for that. The crutches made life difficult, but it also made a hell of an improvement to being an invalid in bed or in a wheelchair. He had to make note of these tiny stages of success. If you didn't mark every one, they were easy to miss. Then it wouldn't feel like you were making any progress at all.

He'd been grateful, so grateful to get into a wheelchair, so he could buzz around independently. But, when he got out of the wheelchair and onto the crutches, standing upright—like homo sapiens were meant to be—was something completely different. He'd loved it for a long time. Yet, all of a sudden, his crutches just weren't enough. And he found himself struggling with that too.

It seemed, once you got something you wanted, you turned around and wanted something else. He was pretty sure it was human nature that made him so contrary, but, at the same time, it was also human nature to reach for something, to achieve it, and then to create a new goal and to reach for that. He just had to make sure he kept reaching. Because pretty darn soon, if he didn't make an effort, he would stop reaching, and he didn't dare do that. He was trying hard to progress.

However, his continued lack of sleep each night was killing him.

And somehow he had to get rid of those damn nightmares. And the guilt.

That ever-residing guilt.

Slowly moving, he stood, wavering ever-so-slightly, using the table for support. Then he grabbed his crutches and wobbled back down the hallway to his room.

He stopped, thinking he heard that voice again. He moved forward ten feet to where two hallways joined up and heard it again. Then he walked forward a step, yet leaned back. He looked down both hallways and saw Dani and Caitlin at the front reception area, standing with another woman. The same tall dark-haired one he'd seen earlier. They were talking together, but he didn't recognize the one woman's voice.

Then again the women were laughing, not whispering in the dead of night. The nearby office door read Accountant. Obviously this unknown woman wasn't his cleaning lady. Not here in the middle of the day. Not here chatting with other office workers. Something was wrong here. His feelings and hopes dashed, he slowly turned and walked back down the hallway.

He didn't know who his cleaning lady was, but he sure wished she'd come back, if only for him to get another good night's sleep.

# Chapter 9

H AILEE LOOKED UP to see Caitlin standing at Hailee's doorway but looking down the hall at something. Caitlin stepped out of sight, and Hailee could hear Caitlin speaking with somebody else. Frowning, Hailee hopped up to see Caitlin talking with one of the patients. Hailee smiled and headed back into her office. When Caitlin reappeared a few minutes later, Hailee looked up and asked, "Problem?"

"No, I don't think so," Caitlin said with a shrug. "But he seemed hesitant to come forward, and I didn't want him to feel like he couldn't talk to us if he needed something."

"Of course not," Hailee said in surprise. "What was he looking for?"

"He didn't really say," she said. "I saw him earlier. He was walking down our hallway, as if listening to something. And then he seemed to shrug and turned around and moved on."

"Maybe he was looking to see if Dani was here?"

"Maybe," Caitlin said, looking relieved at the suggestion.

"As long as he knows he can talk to us anytime, it's all good," Hailee said, comfortably digging back into the pile of work on her desk, smiling to realize she had, indeed, settled in here. It had taken a few days, but Dani had quickly dumped a stack of paperwork on top of Hailee's desk. Hailee was doing a combination of pure bookkeeping work as well as accounting, but she was good with that.

As Dani cleaned off her desk, more and more was getting dumped on Hailee. Her day was quickly filling up. Plus the bookkeeping was behind in terms of producing proper documentation needed for Dani's next investors' meeting with the bank. Hailee would take a few days getting all that taken care of too.

But, all in all, she settled in much better than she had expected. She reached for another stack of invoices, studied them, and shook her head. These were from weeks ago and should have been entered around the same time. It just went to show how quickly the work ran away on Dani. She should have hired an accountant a while back. Had Hailee known she was ready to tackle this job on the level Dani needed, Hailee would have jumped at the chance earlier.

As far as her meals were concerned, she took to that like a fish took to water. Three meals a day was something she hadn't had in a long time. Most of her clothing hung on her shoulders and thin frame now. She used to have a good twenty extra pounds on her long before Jacob was born. After that, it just melted off. So she could stand to gain a little bit, but she wanted more muscle. So she couldn't just eat cinnamon buns. She'd have a thicker layer of excess padding around her instead. Much better that she ate a little bit more in the calorie department as to the healthier foods, indulging in cinnamon rolls occasionally, and went for long walks.

So far, Dennis had treated her almost like a best friend— or maybe his role was more of a mother hen because he came along and watched over her all the time. He would even come to her office, once he found out where she was, if she didn't show up for lunch. Speaking of which, her stomach started to grumble. She looked out her office at Caitlin to find her working, head down, dealing with the phones and schedules, trying to sort out some of the day trips that were happening. Plus they had a bunch of deliveries that would come here and others that Robert would drive into town and pick up. Hailee decided she'd finish one of her stacks, and then she'd take a break and get some breakfast.

As soon as she had that work completed, she got up, walked toward Caitlin, and said, "I'm getting some food. Do you want me to bring you anything?"

Caitlin looked up, distracted, then shook her head until she realized what Hailee had asked. "No," Caitlin said. "I ate early this morning. I'll have a snack and then call it quits a little bit early today too. Heading into town for a dentist appointment."

"Ouch," Hailee said. It had been so long since she'd even made it to the dentist that she probably needed to go in for a checkup herself. But not until the bills slowed down.

"Well, we get that covered here," Caitlin said, "so I figured I should at least take care of my teeth while I can."

At that, Hailee stopped, looked at her, and asked in a low whisper, "We get dental here?"

Caitlin looked up in surprise, then nodded quickly. "Yes. You might even get a better plan too," she said. "I know I was amazed when I found out I could go in and get checkups and even cleaning covered. I think it's two cleanings a year and one checkup or something like that. Believe me. It's more than I've ever had, so I'll take advantage of it."

Hailee thought about it as she walked all the way to the cafeteria. She didn't know the last time she had had any dental coverage. As such, she took good care of her teeth because she couldn't afford to have anything go wrong.

When she entered the large cafeteria, she realized it was almost ten o'clock, and the patients would probably be coming for coffee. She looked to see if any breakfast food was left. A lot of the trays were gone, leaving mostly sweets. She walked through, looking for anything not too sugary.

Dennis caught sight of her and walked up. "You missed breakfast, didn't you?"

She smiled and nodded. "For some reason, I thought maybe there would be some leftovers."

"There is," he said. "What would you like?"

She thought about it and shrugged. "A little bit of fruit, yogurt, and granola would be nice."

"Coming right up," he said and disappeared without asking any details.

She frowned at that, but he came right back with two large parfait glasses layered with something delicious-looking. She stared at both and said, "I didn't want anything too sweet though."

"These are plain Greek yogurt with fresh berries and granola," he said. "I make them up a couple times a week, and these two happen to be what was left." She looked at him and hesitated. He held them up and said, "Raspberry or blueberry?"

"Raspberry," she said instantly. Then she accepted it, looking at it with a smile. "You're sure it's healthy?"

"Of course it's healthy. No extra sugar added. It doesn't need it."

She smiled and nodded. "This should hold me until lunch."

"It will," he said. "You can always have an early lunch too."

"Right," she said with a smile. Then she stepped back

and made herself a small pot of tea at the drinks station. With a fresh cup on the side, she carried her tray back. As she headed across the cafeteria though, she stopped and viewed the massive deck outside in the sun. She'd seen it before but had yet to make it out there. She wandered outside, knowing that she should go back to her office, yet she caught sight of the pool and the hot tub below. Again, things that she had seen but hadn't really taken in. Down below, she could see men put through the paces by their therapists, while other men wandered around with crutches, talking to people in wheelchairs.

A great social atmosphere came with this place, almost as if everyone was part of a large extended family. Hathaway House didn't have any hospital feel or look to it, and she appreciated that. She couldn't imagine anything worse for these guys. She didn't think they could either. A certain sense of freedom was here, and she loved that.

As she looked down, one man with dark hair leaned against the edge of the hot tub. He looked exhausted. She frowned as she studied him and then realized that maybe it wasn't exhaustion on his face but pain. She hesitated, put her tray on the table, and leaned over the railing to see if anybody was with him. He opened his eyes and looked up at her. She stared down and gave him a half smile and then pulled back. She didn't want to seem like she was interfering or being nosy. Yet there was something about him.

Dennis came outside with a big dishcloth and started wiping down the tables. "I thought you would take that back to your office."

She hesitated, then nodded, and said, "I haven't been out on the deck in the sun, so I'm taking five to just sort it out." She pointed over the railing. "I also hadn't taken time to really see the pool or the hot tub."

"Wow," he said, "you are missing something."

He joined her at the corner, and she stopped and stared at what was in his arms. "What is that?"

"Not *what* is that," he said. "It's who. This is Chickie."

He walked closer, and he held a tiny pet bed and inside was one of the smallest animals she'd ever seen. "Oh my." A short tail wagged at her tone, and she reached out a gentle hand and scratched his tiny head.

"His back legs are paralyzed," Dennis said. "He often sits up front with Caitlin, but he has had a couple rough days, so I often keep him in the back with me when that happens."

"Is he better back there?"

"Chances are somebody gave him food he shouldn't have," Dennis said. "Chickie's stomach is very delicate. One of the rules we have is that nobody's allowed to feed any of the animals. They're all on strict diets."

He motioned to the pasture, where she could see the big Newfoundlander. She'd seen it from a distance before but hadn't met him yet.

"I've been here three days on the day shift," she announced, "and I haven't seen any of the dogs."

"They're all around, but you're so tied to your desk," he said. Then he stopped and nodded. "You were doing the cleaning before, weren't you? They would have all gone to their beds. We don't leave them to run around at night."

"In that case," she said, "I'll have to go make everybody's acquaintance."

He smiled and said, "Well, you've just met Chickie. We also have a big Maine Coon around here with three legs, and I know that Stan has been working hard at getting another cat trained to be a therapy cat."

"That'd be a heck of a job," she said. "I can't imagine any cat allowing itself to be trained for anything."

He chuckled. "Absolutely. And I'm not sure this cat will be prepared to do anything, but he's incredibly intuitive, according to Stan."

She hesitated.

"You've never met Stan either, have you?"

She shook her head.

"Well, why don't you leave that tray here, and we'll come back for it in a minute?"

"Or I eat it right now," she said, "and then we go."

"Well," he nodded and said, "sit down. I'll finish my cleaning, and then I'll take you down and introduce you to Stan."

She frowned and glanced back at the offices.

"Stan is part of the office workers here. You should meet him."

"If you say so," she said. "I just don't want to get into trouble."

He laughed. "Dani should have introduced you right away, but I know she's really busy with these meetings."

"She is," she said. "And honestly I'm the one prepping her documents for those meetings, so I'll take a rain check. But maybe this afternoon?"

"Absolutely. Whenever you have time."

She picked up her tray and headed back, but her mind was full of animals and Stan. If she'd only known, she would have been there on day one.

HEATH WASN'T SURE who it was that he'd seen up on the

deck, but it looked like the woman from one of the offices. He shifted in the water and slowly pulled himself out, so he now sat on the edge of the hot tub. He looked around, and Shane came toward him with a couple towels.

"Enough for the day?"

"Yeah, I think so," Heath said. Beside Shane was the big Newfoundlander dog. Heath reached out a hand and called out, "Hey, Helga, come on, girl."

Helga raced over and jumped up so her paws were on the back of the hot tub which gave Heath so much more access for belly scratches.

He cuddled her gently. "You're so fortunate to be here," he said. "Do you know how many welcoming hands there are here for you?"

Helga barked in his face. Heath smiled and looked at Shane. "You're lucky too that you get to have these guys around your workplace."

"Hathaway House is very unusual that way," Shane said with a nod. "But it also works out very well. These animals need a lot of care and attention too. So we rehab both here. Plus I think the animals benefit from all the humans being around, just like the humans benefit from all the animals being around." As he looked past the hot tub, he saw Stan leading the small llama outside again. Shane called out, "Is she okay?"

Stan looked over and raised a hand and said, "She's fine. I was just checking her hooves, but she's doing great." Then he opened up the paddock to lead her inside and took the harness off her face and let her go. Up close was a multicolored horse waiting for the llama. Immediately the two raced off together and then stopped and cuddled up.

Heath stared and smiled. "You don't see that too often."

"No, but now they're both fixtures here," Shane said.

With one towel wrapped around his shoulders now, Heath used the other one to dry off and then slowly turned so his legs were out of the water. "The animals really add another element."

"I think more animals are coming," Shane said. "Oddly enough, I think one comfort animal is a pygmy pig."

Heath stopped, turned, looked at Shane, and asked, "Seriously?"

"Not only does Dani collect strays," Shane said with a head shake and a broad grin, "but so does Stan. Sometimes we're all asked to help out, depending on what the problem is. We had an injured female lab give birth here, but she needed surgery herself, so we had to bottle-feed her pups until she was capable again."

"That would have been fun," he said. "I could get behind something like that." He looked over at Helga, who seemed to immediately realize he was a soft touch, so she dropped her head on his lap. "The only problem," he said, "is how do you keep the facilities clean when these guys are shedding hair everywhere?"

"Which is why we have such a high level of cleaning in the place," Shane said. "And all the filters in the pool and the hot tub specially filter out the hair because we can't keep the animals out of the water."

He looked at the pool, then at Helga, and asked, "Does she swim?"

"Don't even say that word," Shane said hurriedly. "Given half a chance, she jumps in on her own. We've got her mostly trained, so she doesn't go in without an invitation, but an invitation is something that she tends to take on herself."

"Right," he said. "I wouldn't mind being in the pool myself."

"How much swimming have you done since your accident?"

"None," Heath said, staring at the water. He was just hot and sweaty enough from the hot tub that a cool dip in the pool was enticing. "You got any problem with me going in it?"

"Go for it," Shane said. He walked over to Heath's crutches and brought them to him. "But I don't want you to exhaust yourself."

"No, I already did that with you this morning."

Shane chuckled. "Let's get you into the water, if that's where you want to be."

Carefully, moving slowly on the wet cement, they made it to the side of the tiled pool. Heath handed off his crutches and just let his body fall forward. As soon as the water closed over his head, he happily sunk to the bottom. When he slowly surfaced, Shane stood there, watching him with a frown on his face.

"I'm fine," Heath said.

"Well, you looked like you were just a solid slab of meat when you fell in."

"This is so nice," he said. "I used to be a hell of a swimmer. It's been a long time though."

"Swim away," Shane said. "You've got about ten minutes. After that, you're done."

And Heath took Shane for his word.

Heath immediately broke into a front crawl, feeling his body roll with the unused muscle motions. He was surprised to find just how sore he was. His arm didn't quite fully go up and over, so his form sucked. Both legs kicked, but he only had one foot, so one leg was active, and the other one just felt like it was sticking out there doing nothing. It was such an odd feeling, but he was mobile, and he was doing it on his own. He raced forward to one side and then back to the other. By the time he had completed three full laps, he could feel his energy waning. He pulled into the shallow end and sat on the step, just catching his breath.

Shane walked up beside him. "And?"

"Well, it felt good to swim and to support myself in the water without needing crutches," he said, "but it really reminded me that I'm not in the shape I used to be in and that the muscles don't want to go in the direction they're supposed to go."

Shane grinned. "Isn't that the truth? But now that you've been in here, and I see that you can swim, I'll incorporate it into your weekly workouts."

"I'm okay with that." Heath looked over at the hot tub, then at Shane, and asked, "Are we done for the morning, or is there more?"

"No, you're done, but I want you in your room now, so I can take a look at your back."

"Great. I thought I could hop in the hot tub a bit longer."

Shane shook his head. "No, your energy level is already way too low. We may have to use a wheelchair to get you to your room as it is. The crutches would be hard with your current energy levels."

As he looked at the crutches, the rest of his energy started to drain, making him realize how tired he really was. Heath nodded. "I'm afraid you're right. I didn't even realize it until now."

At that, Shane walked over to the side and grabbed one

of the many waiting wheelchairs, then pulled it over, and said, "This time I'll take you up. Next time you're on your own."

# Chapter 10

SEVERAL DAYS LATER Hailee started to get to know and to identify the different staff members and patients. During her night shift work of cleaning, she didn't get to meet very many people. But now any number of individuals came through the offices at any given time. It was one of the oddest feelings. When she had started her cleaning job, she'd been so grateful to Dani but hadn't really recognized how different it was to work here on the day shift as compared to working the night shift.

She saw very few people at night. If she ever saw even three in her entire shift, she'd have been surprised. But now that she had this daytime job, dozens of people were coming and going all the time. The other job had had a sense of privacy, something she'd been happy to have at the time. Yet now, she felt like she was part of something. She was involved in the hustle and bustle of daily life here at Hathaway House.

She'd been included. Maybe that was what was different. This kind of felt like she belonged.

Cleaning in the nights almost felt like she was whispering silently through the halls, not letting anybody know she was here. And now it was a completely different thing. She was slowly getting to know more of the staff, and, of course, some of the patients came up with headaches of their own.

Usually about paperwork or phone calls or connections and appointments that they needed to make and couldn't get made on their own without some help or maybe needed to go into town. So patients were continually talking to the women at the front desk if not with Dani and Hailee.

It was interesting. Hailee had her own office and a door that she could close, if and when she needed the privacy to get the work done. And yet, with it open, she was still part of the inner circle of how everything operated. A very different feeling than she'd had at night. However, one thing was missing.

And she didn't even know his name.

She'd gone past his door several times and hesitated, wanting to go in and to say hi but had struggled with that. She felt like she'd be interfering, an interloper in some ways, or maybe he didn't want to see who she was. If their positions were reversed, she'd be feeling bereft and deserted if the cleaning lady had abandoned her. *Abandoned.* And that just made her wince because was there any worse feeling in the world? She didn't think so. She'd been there and had experienced the same thing herself, and it was crippling in a way.

A couple conversations happened outside her office that were low-key, and she hadn't been invited to join in, so she hadn't a clue what was going on. But it was odd. She kept her ear perked out of curiosity but never really heard too much. She heard the name *Heath*, which made her think of moors and long walks with dogs and walking sticks. The broody type of male. But she didn't have any real basis for that kind of an intuitive image.

As she kept working away through the accounts and cleaning up matters, checking things out and making sure everything was up to date, Dani stopped in and looked at her with half a smile, then asked, "Have you got a moment?"

Hailee smiled and said, "For you, always." Dani came in and closed the door and sat down. The fact that she'd closed the door immediately put Hailee on edge. "Is there a problem?" she asked lightly. But inside, her stomach screamed. Dear God, she so didn't want to lose this job.

"No, no, no," Dani said, immediately shaking her head. "Sorry. I didn't mean to make it seem like this was a big deal." She turned to glance at the door, then frowned. "But I guess, by shutting the door, that would be an immediate assumption, wouldn't it?"

"I don't know enough about how this place works yet to know if it's a problem or not," Hailee said, "but almost every instance where the boss comes in and shuts the door tends to make employees cringe."

"Well," Dani said with a half smile, "this is something different."

Hailee sat back. "What's up?"

"First," Dani said, "how do you fit in?"

"Well," Hailee said. "Surprisingly well."

"Good," Dani said with a self-satisfied smile. "I knew you'd be perfect for here."

"And how would you know that?" Hailee smiled. "We've been friends for a long time, but I don't know that we've ever really worked together."

"No, but I understand who you are inside," she said. "And I'm so sorry for all the trauma you've been through."

Hailee's smile fell away. She stared at the papers in front of her, but she nodded. "Thank you. It's one of those things that life throws at you that you have to walk through alone, and nobody can really help you emotionally. Even if hands reach out to give you some assistance, they can't walk in your shoes with you," she said, raising her gaze. "It took me a long time to realize that and to just buckle in and ride through it."

"You might not have anybody who can walk in your shoes," Dani said gently, "but it doesn't mean having people walking beside you can't make the journey easier."

"Very true," Hailee said with a half smile. "Unfortunately the person who should have been there for me wasn't."

Dani nodded again. "Sometimes I think we're destined to go through really crappy relationships so that, when we do find something special, we recognize it."

Hailee looked at her in surprise. "Well, that's a different take on it. Here I thought we were supposed to find something special right off the bat and set ourselves up for life. Isn't that what we're taught? To get an education, get married, have kids, and be the perfect wife?"

"There's no such thing as perfection," Dani said. "And I don't think our mothers knew a whole lot more than we did at our age either." She sighed. "The generations aren't getting more stupid. I think they're getting smarter," she admitted. "But people are changing, expectations on relationships are changing, and the role models and what each brings to the table are changing. So it's a case of finding what works for you and only you."

"And have you found it?" Hailee asked quietly. She'd heard an awful lot of good things about Aaron but hadn't actually met the man.

Dani beamed. "Yes," she said. "Finally. But, like you, I went through a rough time first. But I'm pretty confident that what Aaron and I have will go the distance. Anyway, that's not why I came here."

"Okay," Hailee said, slowly crossing her hands as she

placed them on top of her desk, so she could sit tall and focus on Dani. "What's up?

"One of our patients," Dani said, "and I'm just hearing about this now, was wondering who the cleaning lady was who's disappeared."

Hailee's eyebrows rose. "Interesting," she said. She turned slightly to look out the window on her left. "Is his room down that short hallway that leads to one of the fire exits? On the left-hand side?" she said, closing her eyes. "I think it's the first of three doors?"

Dani, her voice rich with laughter, said, "Exactly. That's him."

Hailee smiled. "I wondered if he'd miss me."

At that, Dani's eyebrows shot up. "So tell me more," she said. "What's going on between the two of you?"

Hailee shook her head. "Nothing, honestly. But I used to mop that hallway last every night that I cleaned," she said with a small deprecating smile. "And he used to wake up about that time." She laughed, then sobered. "One time I thought I heard him cry out. I knocked on the door and poked my head around the corner to see if he needed some assistance. After that, we spoke several times. Not too often."

"Well, his name is Heath," she said. "Heath Hankerson. He was asking about you, and now I understand why. He's struggling to sleep."

"He said that he had a hard time sleeping. The drugs weren't agreeing with him, and they left him groggy and brain foggy, so he hated taking them because of the way they made him feel."

Dani nodded. "It's amazing just how many of the drugs these men react to," she said sadly. "They come out of the hospitals—often heavily drugged on pain pills, sleeping aids, antibiotics, and any number of medications required to survive their surgeries—and then they go one way or the other. They develop a supersensitivity to some of them, or they find they can't survive without them. And they need stronger and stronger drugs."

"Well, I definitely got the impression that Heath went the other way," Hailee said.

"Yes," Dani said with a nod. "That's exactly right. So he struggles with taking any sleeping medication."

"I've never seen who he is," Hailee said with a chuckle. "His room was always dark, and I only had more or less ambient lighting in the hallway, just from the night-lights while I was mopping. I tried to keep the lights turned down. A little harder to see that way, but, as long as you're method-ical, you know you've reached every corner anyway."

Dani nodded. "Now that I know who he's talking about and why he wants to know what happened to you," Dani said rising, "I'll go talk to him myself."

"Are you short a cleaner?"

"Yes," Dani said, "but you're not going back to that."

"What difference does it make?" Hailee said with a smile. "I mean, I worked a full-time job and then came here and worked too."

"Yes," she said. "But a lot of laws regulate something like that within the same company, and you don't need to do both jobs now. Remember? That was the reason for pulling those two wages together to give you this job."

Hailee bit her lip and nodded. "I understand," she said. "I just feel bad for him."

"I'll talk to his therapist and see if we can come up with something else to help him sleep through the night." And with that, she opened the door and left it wide open and disappeared down the hallway.

All Hailee could think about was the name Heath and the man himself, wondering if she should dare visit him and say hi. Yet, after Dani's visit, Hailee felt it would be much better to keep her distance.

HEATH SAT ON the edge of his bed, rubbing his eyes. He'd just woken up from a short power nap. He hated the damn sleeping pills he was forced to take, but, without sleep, he couldn't function at all. So it had been a painful compromise. But not one he liked. It didn't seem fair that he should have to use drugs to get the rest his body needed. He was exhausted inside and out, so why the heck couldn't this work out better for him?

When he heard a knock on his door, he called out, "Come in." He looked up to see Dani standing in the doorway. He glared at her. "Is there a problem?"

She laughed. "Nope, not at all," she said. "But I hear you've been asking about one of my staff."

His frown deepened. "And?"

She took several more steps into the room. "Are you always this grumpy or just when you don't get sleep?"

He glanced at the bed behind him. "I just woke up from a nap," he said, "so I should be getting sleep."

"But apparently you're not," she said quietly.

He didn't look at her this time. Instead he twisted and gently collapsed on the bed, wincing at the unnatural movement. "I keep trying to," he said, staring up at the ceiling. "But I don't seem able to."

"You're having trouble sleeping, or, when you wake up,

you're having trouble going back to sleep?"

"Going back to sleep," he said. "I figured it's exhaustion that gets me under in the first place. It wears off, and my body sleeps enough that it's looking to wake up and do something else."

"Is there a connection to this cleaning lady?"

He stiffened and then glared at Dani. "I didn't say that," he growled.

"Okay," she said, "then tell me why you want to know anything about her."

He just shrugged.

"Well, I'll hardly give you any information," she said, as she walked a little closer, "unless you tell me something too."

He gave her a small wave of his hand. "It doesn't matter," he said. "She's probably gone anyway."

"Yes, and no," Dani said.

He rolled his head to the side and stared at her. "That sounds very evasive."

"Actually it's not," she said. "She's still here but in a different capacity."

"Why? Did she not like cleaning?"

"She had other skills that we needed a little more," Dani admitted.

"Of course," he said. "Everybody else is important." What he left unsaid was everybody *except for him*. And then realized he was being a petulant child. "Well, hopefully she's happy." If she had another job, then she wasn't coming back, and that meant he would have to find a solution to his sleepless problem one way or the other. He didn't know what he was supposed to do, and exhaustion was dragging him down and affecting his performance in all aspects. He couldn't even eat properly. His stomach was continually churning up in knots.

"Would it help if she came and talked to you?"

He shook his head. "No," he said harshly. "She's already moved on, so whatever."

Dani hesitated.

He glared at her. "If there's nothing else …"

She nodded quietly. "I'll talk to you about it later then." And she turned and walked out, closing the door quietly behind her.

He wanted to say, *Don't bother. Absolutely nothing to talk about.* Because obviously the woman wouldn't be cleaning at two in the morning anymore, so what difference did it make? He groaned and scrubbed his face. "You'll have to deal with this one way or the other," he said to himself. Sleep and nightmares went hand in hand. He had tried a lot of different things, but nothing seemed to work. And now that he'd had enough sleep to make it through the rest of the day, he knew there was no point in trying right now.

When someone knocked again, he groaned and called out, "Come in."

A petite woman entered. She smiled at him and said, "I'm setting up yoga classes. Does that hold any interest for you?"

He shook his head. "I doubt Shane would even allow me to go to the class, at least not yet. I don't bend like a pretzel very well."

"Well, the idea of a yoga class," she said, "would be to start at whatever level you're capable of moving at and then stretching and moving toward improving that range of motion."

"If it requires anything more than lying in bed or sitting in a wheelchair," he said quietly, "you've already maxed out my range of motion."

She gave him a bright smile. "Not quite," she said. "I've seen you in the pool, so I know you can do some stuff."

He glared at her, but her smile stayed in place. Finally he groaned and said, "At nighttime, I have a hard time sleeping, so that'll probably just rev me up."

"No," she said. "One of the reasons that we do yoga is to help people sleep, so they don't need sleep aids."

At that, he snapped, "Did Dani set you up for this?"

"Well, Dani is my boss," she said with a laugh. "We thought maybe there would be enough interest in yoga classes to run a couple."

"Well, let me know how it goes," he said. And then he slowly shifted and rolled over toward the window. "Close the door on your way out, please." He waited to listen for her footsteps as she exited his room and heard the door slowly closing. With that *snick* of the door, he allowed himself to relax.

"And now what the hell am I supposed to do?" he muttered. "You're miserable inside and out." And that just made him feel worse.

# Chapter 11

A FTER SEVERAL MORE days Hailee finally decided that she couldn't stand not knowing for sure if they were talking about the same patient. She knew they were, … but that niggling doubt remained. She got up and walked down the hallway and got the room number. She should have done this a long time ago. Then she came back, and, as she did so, she asked Caitlin, "Heath's in Room 221, correct?"

Caitlin quickly glanced through her files and nodded. "Yes, that's correct." She looked over at her and said, "Problem?"

Hailee smiled and shook her head. "No, I just needed to check it for our records." She walked back into her office and sat down, wondering if she should set up a meeting with him. She was bound to see him sometime but didn't want to come face-to-face with him unexpectedly. But every time she'd been in that area when mopping, she couldn't see his face. So, whether that was a good thing or a bad thing, she didn't know.

It *had* put him in the mystery-man category. And the mystery man was almost perfect for her. Yet she didn't want to deal with any more men who wouldn't be real—that had been her husband. Unfortunately now she was sitting here, thinking that mystery men were probably perfect precisely because they *weren't* real. She had had enough of reality. At the same time, her mystery man was also a fantasy, and she didn't need that. But it was nice to have, and it stopped her from feeling lonely.

She still needed to recognize who he was, so she didn't come upon him unexpectedly and not realize it was him. But she wasn't sure how to do it. She could ask Dani, but that felt wrong now, after Heath had been asking about her. Hailee wouldn't sit there and haunt his hallway either because that felt worse. So how else was she supposed to know? There would be photos in their patient files, but that felt intrusive, like she shouldn't be looking there without good reason. All in all, that thought made it a little creepy. She had to do something about it, but she just didn't know what. She put it off yet again.

As she headed into dinner that night, she was once again amazed at how much her life had simplified by being here. With Dani giving her residency here, that meant Hailee's food and board was free, freeing up more of her paychecks. Although she hadn't had one yet, it would be automatically deposited into her bank account. And, maybe for the first time, since she could eat enough now, she could reduce her own stress levels.

As she walked up to the cafeteria line, she was happy to see that she'd timed it just about right. She'd been working later these last few days to get caught up and to get Dani's books all ready for the big meeting she had coming up. In the meantime, Hailee had allowed most of the dinnertime crowd to go through first, and she left afterward to have hers. It was after six now, and about eight people were in front of her with various forms of mobility. She loved that here too. Nobody was in a rush, and everybody was entitled to take as much time as they needed to get from point A to point B.

Sometimes people helped. Yet sometimes they didn't, and it was a case of just watch and hope that the patients made it without crashing. Other times though, multiple people all moved as a large group. And she loved that too. Loved the camaraderie and the friendships she'd witnessed here. She never heard any grumbling in the line. Everybody was joking or teasing others. Dani worked hard to keep the positive atmosphere here.

Dani had done a phenomenal job, but the more it grew, the harder it would be to keep this way. Hailee didn't know how much of a warning everybody got when they first arrived after being hired on or accepted in, but she couldn't imagine Dani being anything but blunt and open about what her expectations were for people here and what their expectations needed to be for their own progress. Hailee herself hadn't received any such speech, but then she and Dani went way back. They knew who they each were on the inside. Although Dani had had a tough time initially, she'd pulled through and had done an incredible job trying to help everybody else.

For herself, Hailee had seemingly gone the wrong direction and had ended up in more pain than she could have imagined by getting married and getting pregnant. There'd been so much agony that she often forgot about the rest and focused solely on the pain. And maybe she needed to focus more on the good things in her life. She stared aimlessly around her, stopping the line from moving forward. Snapping out of it, she stepped up smartly to see Dennis's big grin.

"What're you doing? Sleeping?" he chided her gently.

"Maybe," she said. "Heavy thoughts, at least."

"Well, you park them right now," he said. "No heavy

thoughts when you're eating my food. Food should bring happiness, not sadness."

She smiled at him. "Well, I hadn't heard that before."

"Well, you're hearing it now," he said. "Food should be a comfort. It should feed the soul and feed the heart, and it should definitely feed the body. Otherwise you're eating the wrong kind of food."

"For so long," she said, "I put food in my mouth because it was available to keep me going."

"Well, your luck has changed," Dennis announced. He motioned to the array of food in front of him. "What can I get you?"

"Vegetables," she said immediately.

He nodded and lifted a lid. There was a beautiful stir-fry with mouth-watering broccoli in some kind of a light sauce.

"That looks lovely," she said. He served her one scoop. As she considered it, and she said, "Three scoops total please." He added two more; now her plate was mostly full.

"What will you have for protein to go with that?" he asked.

She smiled at him. "What have you got?"

"I've got a beautiful piece of sea bass here for you," he said.

"And I'll take it too," she said. "I can't remember the last time I had fish."

He just stared at her, shook his head, and reached for a lovely piece of fish that he placed on the side of her plate. "Now, potatoes, rice, anything else?"

She shook her head. "Nope, nothing. I'll add a green salad as I go through." She was wondering if she would even have room to eat some salad, but it looked good. She knew that they made it fresh every day, everything from Greek to

Caesar. Grabbing a small bowl, she added a Caesar salad to her tray and then moved over, bypassing the coffee and reaching for a large glass of water.

Slowly she made her way outside to the deck, where she sat down all alone. She still hadn't collected any friends who she could have a meal with. She was hoping that that would happen, but so far it hadn't yet. Even as she sat here, she could hear friendly groups forming all around her.

She knew she was new, although not as fresh as anybody suspected, but had hoped that maybe she would have made a little more strides in the friendship area. Perhaps it was her air to stay away. And that's something she had garnered after her husband and she started having a lot of trouble. She hadn't wanted to get into that well of self-pity, where all she could talk about were the problems in her life, so she avoided people until she got her balance back.

But now, as she sat staring out across the hills, she realized she was more than ready to have some friendly conversation.

Almost as if her wish was fulfilled, somebody with a tray, standing on two crutches, stopped at her side.

He looked down at her and asked, "Do you mind if I share your table?"

She looked up at him in surprise and glanced around, then realized that all the tables were full. She immediately shook her head and said, "Not at all. I didn't realize this was the last free table."

"Doesn't matter if you're willing to share," he said with a smile. He placed his tray several seats over from her, as if he wanted space too. But still, at least she wasn't entirely alone. And then she realized that she recognized him from the hot tub the other day. Although maybe not necessarily everybody would have recognized him, for what made it more memorable for her was because he'd been in such pain. His muscles weren't at peace. And she'd seen way too much of that with her own son. She ate quietly, and finally, when she looked up, she caught him staring at her and glancing at her plate.

"You eat only vegetables?"

"Sometimes," she admitted. "I missed out on all the fresh vegetables for a long enough time. And I know for a fact I need the nutrition to get my body back to what it needs to be."

At that, curiosity piqued his gaze. "You don't look sick."

"No?" she said. "That's the thing in a place like this. The people who are physically injured are reasonably visible. The rest of us have our own problems, only they aren't as visible."

"Yeah? What kind of problem are you dealing with?" And there was almost a derisive tone to it.

She immediately felt her walls coming up. "Nothing much. Just long-term stress. And I'm smart enough to know I need my nutrients to help get back over the hump of what that does to you."

He nodded. "Sorry. I didn't mean to pry. In a place like this, you tend to forget—just because you're not missing an arm or a leg or your back isn't all gimped up or you're not carrying around half-a-dozen steel plates in your body that add ten pounds to your frame—that the people who work here can also have problems. And, of course, we all do. We just don't like to acknowledge them."

His apology surprised her. She looked at him and gave him a quick nod, then said, "It's not an issue. I just feel bad even complaining when I work here, and everybody is triumphing, overcoming such incredible challenges."

"Sometimes some people are overcoming more than others," he said, his lips turning down in the corners.

"Anybody who is here," she said, "anybody who's trying to survive, they deserve all the kudos coming their way. It's not easy to work with people who are struggling, and it's not easy to be somebody who's got a problem which seems insurmountable in my own head, but it really isn't because I see how much you guys are growing and changing. In fact, you're my role models. Don't ever think less of yourself for the journey that you're taking right now."

His eyes widened slightly, and he looked at her with a tilt to his head, as if she were unique or maybe odd.

She shrugged. "I know," she said. "I'm not normal."

"Nothing is normal," he said. "Not in this life. We are all who we are, but we don't usually learn these substantial lessons until we get through some of life's worst difficulties."

"Yes," she said, "I can agree with that. And I'm finding a lot of hidden benefits to being here that I hadn't realized originally. As if seeing what you are all working on is showing me where I need to work on things too." And it was surprising that she understood the truth of her own words. If she hadn't come here, she would have been wallowing in her personal losses and in her own grief, finding it very difficult to pick up her feet and to move forward. Instead she'd started to see the changes in her perspective. She still had a lot to work on, but it was a start. "It's the best thing I ever did, coming here," she said.

And, with that, she picked up a large piece of broccoli and put it into her mouth.

"INTERESTING WAY TO look at life," he said. Heath looked

down at his plate. It was heavy in starches but also heavy in protein. But hers was full of bright colorful vegetables, and he realized she was right. A lot more nutrients were available to him that he wasn't taking advantage of, mostly because he was a meat-and-potatoes kind of guy. But that didn't mean he shouldn't be helping himself to the vitamins and minerals that were on offer. He glanced back at the cafeteria line and realized how much farther he would have to go just to get some veggies. Next time would be soon enough.

"Is there something I can get you?" she asked.

He looked at her in surprise and then shook his head. "No, not at all," he said. "I can't eat much more than this anyway."

"So what were you thinking of then?"

"I thought you were right," he said. "I haven't really eaten much in the way of vegetables, and I'm sure my body needs it. And even supplements, which I do take, aren't the same as getting the vitamins and minerals that I really need from food."

"If you want me to get you a bowl of vegetables, just say the word," she said. "I'd be happy to."

"Nah," he said, hating to put anybody out.

She looked at him and frowned. "Are you one of those tough guys who can't ask for help?"

His gaze narrowed at her.

She just beamed a bright smile. "Not that I know anything about men like that …"

That surprised a laugh out of him. "In a place like this," he said, "I imagine we all are guilty of that problem." He watched as her lips pinched together. And then he gave a clipped nod. "You too, I suppose." And his shoulders relaxed, as she nodded.

"Exactly. Me too. I keep trying to accept help when it's offered, but it's hard. You shut people out, you keep them on the outside, not wanting them to see the depths of your pain and your confusion and what you've been through because you know that they can't even begin to walk in your shoes."

"I think the fact that we walk in our own shoes," he said, "is what gives us our own unique perspective in life. You certainly don't want anybody else to walk in your shoes. Sure, we provide them with some empathy into our situation, but you don't want them to suffer like you have. You just want them to walk in their own shoes and to handle their own challenges with their heads up, knowing they're not alone."

She sagged back and looked at him. "That's very prophetic."

He shrugged. "I have my moments. And, on that note," he said, "I'll ask you if you would mind getting me a bowl of whatever that mixed veggie dish is. Because I should be eating vegetables."

She laughed, hopped to her feet, and headed back to the cafeteria line.

He smiled as he watched her. Tall, superslim—as in too thin—with long dark hair and a smile on her face. A smile of somebody who had earned it. Somebody who'd walked through the trials of life and had come out on the other side with more inner calm. She might think that she hadn't gotten very far in life, but he could see the challenges she had surpassed. The milestones marked her actual growth.

Almost like people should have rings like trees, so you could see the maturity on the inside and not just on the outside. It would help to match people's ages up with their own growth. Not that he wanted people to look old, but he wanted people to recognize that wisdom didn't always come on an easy pathway or just from the passage of time. Mostly it happened after hard years of journeys on steep paths that were convoluted and from decisions that maybe were better taken a different way.

But nevertheless, after you've traveled that path, and you've come to the other side, there you are, standing proud and firm. Yes, looking a little more aged and a little worse for wear in some cases, but these signs weren't something that you should hide with makeup or whatever. They were wrinkles in maybe a thicker skin that you should wear with pride. Not to show everybody and boast, *Look at what I've done*, but to know that you have surmounted that challenge, and that it was something worth going through as you now stand on the other side from a position of strength. These were the trials and tribulations of this thing called the human condition.

Wouldn't it be nice if any of that came with warnings, like in roadside alerts, that said, *Hey, if you didn't want to do any of this, then you shouldn't have come to this pathway?* When we started this journey, we needed the reminder that it could change in a heartbeat. Just like it had for him. And he suspected that that was a very similar issue for her too.

Just then, she came back toward him with not a small bowl but a large bowl of bright green veggies in her hand. She smiled at him. "You do need colorful veggies," she said, "but what you desperately need is dark greens. So here's a mix."

He looked at it. "Your bowl is brighter," he said, as he studied some of the steamed veggies before him. "I don't even know what some of this is."

"Try it," she said. "And then I'll tell you what they are."

He hesitated but then realized that she was watching him, her own gaze narrowed but with laughter in her eyes. He sighed. "I did ask you to get them for me, didn't I?"

"You absolutely did," she said. "And remember. What we take, we eat."

"You could eat most of this," he muttered.

She shook her head. "Nope. You try it first."

He picked up something that looked a whole lot like spinach but tougher and took a bite. He frowned, but the flavor was rich and deep, and, as he chewed, he thought it wasn't all that bad. When he caught her looking at him, he smiled and said, "I don't know what I just ate, but it was pretty decent."

"That was Swiss chard," she said. "Go ahead and try the lighter greenish leaf on the side."

"Spinach, right?" He picked it up and tasted it and frowned. "It's great."

"That was steamed spinach," she said. "And that's not all. You have broccoli and some kohlrabi in there too. That's an unusual thing to add to a dish like this, but it adds hidden depth and density to the plate."

He looked at his bowl and asked, "Which is the kohlra-bi?"

"May I?" she asked as she took his fork, leaned over, and poked part of a slice of a light green stalk with a white end. "Something between a cucumber and a turnip." She returned his fork to him.

He bit it, surprised to find a bit of a crunch to it, and then nodded. "That's really good." He dug in his bowl, found another piece, and popped it into his mouth.

"The rest of that," she said, "you should eat with no trouble."

# Chapter 12

EVEN THOUGH DINNER was over, she carried his words throughout the rest of the day. She still didn't know what his name was, and he didn't wear a name tag. She'd seen name tags on a lot of the patients, but it probably depended on the individual men as to whether they wanted to be identified. As she, herself, didn't particularly care to wear a name tag.

For the next few days, she looked around for him but didn't see him. Then, at dinnertime, she was walking through to the deck, all alone, looking for a place and realized that she'd come out a little too early as the tables were mostly full. Off to the side at a table, all alone, was the same guy. She walked over and said, "Hey. Mind if I join you?"

He looked up at her and smiled. "Absolutely. It's time for me to return the favor," he said and motioned at his table. This time it was only a table for four though, so she sat down across from him slightly to the side. He looked at her and laughed. "So do you have any meat in there?"

She pointed at the two skewers of souvlaki Dennis had given her. "And lots and lots of veggies," she said. In fact, she had this massive Greek salad too. "I gather it's Greek night or something," she added.

"Absolutely," he said. "They do all kinds of food themes

here. And it's pretty impressive."

"I'm quite surprised," she said. "The food is unbelievable."

"It certainly is," he nodded. "But I believe that's part of their actual philosophy here. The food needs to help feed you and restore you to your balance, so it needs to be something that you want to come and eat and not just eat to survive."

"Eat to thrive," she said with a nod of her head. She picked up her spoon and stirred the cup of coffee she had.

"Don't you drink coffee all day long?"

She looked at him in surprise. "Some days I do," she admitted. "But Dennis made me a special coffee tonight," she said, "something Greek."

"Oh," he said, frowning. "I must have missed that."

She smiled up at him. "Really? I don't think you miss much."

He grinned. "Maybe not," he said. "Although I haven't seen you around for very long."

"I've worked here off and on," she said, "for about six weeks total now."

"Good for you," he said. "I'm Heath, by the way."

He caught her just while she was inhaling and taking a bite. She immediately started coughing, and, by the time she was done, he held her a glass of water and looked at her worriedly. She took several deep breaths, then took a sip of water to clear her throat, and then said, "Sorry. Man, that went down the wrong way." She hoped she had covered up her shock at finally seeing who she'd been visiting with at night when on mop duty.

"Are you okay?" The concern was evident on his face and voice.

She smiled, nodded, and said, "That'll teach me. I guess I was a little too hungry."

"Two hatches," he said. "One for air and one for food. Don't mix them up."

At that, she burst out laughing.

He grinned at her. "Haven't you ever heard that before?"

"No," she said, "I haven't."

"Then you don't have any kids either," he said, "because that's something you get to tell them all the time too."

At that, her laughter fell away, and she stared at her bowl. "No," she said. "I don't."

As if sensing that the mood had shifted, he nodded and started working on his plate again.

She continued to eat for several minutes. "How long have you been here?" she asked when she could, trying to restore the camaraderie that had been there before the topic of children was mentioned.

"Too long and yet, not long enough," he said. "Maybe about six weeks. But I'll have another couple months anyway. I've hit a snag and slowed my progress."

"Sometimes you need longer," she said, "but, even from the time I've been here, I've seen some fantastic progress."

"And I have too, in some ways," he said. "And then the hardest things cause you to slip backward, and you just don't know what to do about that."

"I'm sorry," she said. "If there's anything I can do to help, let me know."

"You could give me your name," Heath said.

"Hailee." She smiled. "Is there anything else I can help you with?"

He chuckled. "No it's my burden to bear."

"But remember," she said. "Just because it's your burden

doesn't mean others can't be there to give you a helping hand."

He looked at her appreciatively. "So you did remember our conversation."

"Not only remembered it but I've also thought about it a lot," she said, "because you're right. And some of the pathways that I've taken haven't been the easiest, but they have had their own rewards. I keep forgetting to focus on the rewards and not on what seemed like punishments."

"I think *punishment* says I need to place blame," he said slowly. "And I'm a bad one for that too. Part of my problem is guilt. I feel so guilty for an accident that happened when I was driving that cost the life of my friends. I keep forgetting that I need to rejoice in the fact that I am still alive. And that they didn't suffer."

"I'm sorry," she said sincerely. "Losing someone is not easy."

He looked up at her sharply, his gaze assessing.

She immediately dropped her gaze to her plate. And then her shoulders sagged, and she nodded. "Yes, I've lost somebody too."

"And that's a bond that we don't really want to have," he said quietly. "But we both understand how much of a loss that can be."

Her lips kicked up in the corners, and she nodded, but she didn't answer him. She felt his gaze on her again. She continued to work through her giant bowl of Greek salad. When she was halfway through it, she realized she might have taken too much. "You know what? When you're so hungry," she said, "you just don't how much to serve yourself."

"You don't realize," he said, in a parody of her words,

"that when you're so hungry, you take big bites out of life because you think you can handle it all, but you can't."

She sat back and stared at him. "Where did that come from?"

"I was just sitting here, thinking about how anxious I was to do so much and then thinking that, just because I wanted to do it, I could do it. But I realized just how really big a bite of that plateful I was signing up for."

"Isn't that the point in time where you step back and take smaller bites?" she asked curiously.

He grinned at her. "Is that what you did?"

"No. I fell into this dark bottomless pit. I forgot all about taking bites and handling what was happening in my world and came close to giving up," she admitted.

"So did I, but I think climbing back out of that pit is the lesson here. If you can't jump up and grab the whole thing all at once, you're supposed to do it little by little."

"But little by little, it doesn't feel the same," she murmured.

"No, but the progress is there nonetheless. It's just you can't keep counting on it day to day because the day-to-day progress doesn't show. But, if you were to check in once a week or once a month, you would see a more significant increment, and, therefore, it would be more visible."

"But when it's not measurable?"

"Like dealing with loss? Or guilt?"

She nodded. "Yes, precisely that."

He smiled and said, "You know what? According to what everybody's trying to tell me, that's exactly what we're supposed to do. It's to not look at our achievements and to not grade them on a day-to-day basis but more to acknowledge that we've gotten through another day and hopefully without feeling as guilty as we did the day before."

"I wonder if I'll ever get there."

"I can tell you will. I'm not there yet myself, but I have seen some progress in my own life," he admitted. "But I don't want you to tell anybody about it." He laughed. "Because they might make me sit in more of those therapy sessions." And he scrunched up his face into a comical frown.

She burst out laughing. "Oh my, aren't they the worst?"

He stared at her. "Have you been to any of the ones here though?"

She immediately shook her head. "No. I attended some, and you know something? They were trying to get my head straightened around, but I'm not sure that they even understood that it takes time before you can even see that your head is screwed up. You're so caught up in the loss and the whirlwind of pain that you don't *want* to hear much, and your doors are shut, so you *can't* hear whatever it is they're trying to say."

He leaned back in his chair and studied her for a long moment. "You really do understand, don't you?"

Her lips quirked. "And you have no idea what I'd do to not understand."

"Yes, I do," he said, "because I'm the same."

She dropped her gaze once again to her plate and realized that, although he was the same, his pain was different.

"And I can see that you're trying to separate your pain from mine," he said, leaning across the table, his hand reaching out to cover hers. "That your pain is more personal, that your pain is more intense. And it probably is because it wasn't a husband, a brother, a father, or a child in my case. But they were my two best friends, and they were my bros. I was raised in a foster family, and these were the only two men in my entire life that I ever bonded with. So it felt like having my arms, my legs, and my heart ripped out over and over again every time I woke up to realize that I was alive and that they would never be at my side again."

She could feel the tears forming in the back of her eyes. She stopped and pushed her plate back ever-so-slightly, then pinched the bridge of her nose. Her other hand was still held in his. She squeezed his for a long moment, and he pressed back. When she finally had control of herself, she looked at him and said, "It's probably not a good idea to bond over pain."

"I've got a suggestion then," he said, those large dark eyes of his warming up. "How about we bond over recovering?"

She gave him the smallest of a smile. "I think I can get behind that."

"Good," he said. "Not every day, but maybe every couple days and perhaps once a week, let's check in with each other and see how we're doing."

She took a deep breath. "Maybe," she said, cautious of offering too much of herself.

He smiled. "And, just like me, you're scared and hesitant to get involved because *what happens when we get involved?*" he murmured.

"It hurts when we lose that connection," she said.

"But we know that going in. We understand that both of us have this burden on our backs. And it's not like we can stop or put down that burden immediately. We can't put it down because we'd feel even guiltier, but what we must understand is that our burden doesn't have to have the weight we're giving it. We're assigning that weight to it. But, if we straighten up, we can still acknowledge that we lost part of our life but not let it be the hefty forty pounds on our back that we're continually carrying."

"Wow," she said. "Wouldn't it be nice if we could lighten that load?"

"Is there any reason we can't?" he challenged. "Think about it. We bear the load because we want to. That's what the psychologists around us don't understand. They think that we don't have any option, and we're guilt-stricken. We carry that load because we love those we lost and because we don't ever want to be parted from them."

"Right," she said slowly. "So, in other words, we need to incorporate them more into our life but in a lighter way so that we don't feel the burden."

"Because it isn't a burden," he corrected. "I don't want to let go of my two friends. I imagine one on one shoulder and the other on the other shoulder. The guilt is something I'll have to work through, but I don't want to work through it if it means letting them go."

"And that's what everybody wants us to do. Let them go."

He nodded. "Which is why I haven't made the progress that everybody else wants me to make here," he murmured. "And maybe it's because I also can't reconcile and verbalize what I mean. Of course a lack of sleep isn't helping. I'm cranky and cantankerous."

"Sorry about the lack of sleep. I think you're doing an outstanding job verbally on all this," she said. "And, if you can't tell the psychologist, why don't you write it down? Write how you feel and what it is that you want out of this. And keep your friends so that you can look from your left shoulder to your right shoulder with a smile on your face and can remember how much they meant to you and can still mean to you because you have those memories."

It was his turn to sit back. And then slowly he nodded. "And what do you think? Can we make some kind of a commitment here to help each other?"

She smiled ever-so-slightly. "As long as it's not formal and as long as you understand that if my world blows up ..."

He waved away her protestations. "Everybody's world is blowing up. I'm not talking about forever here. I'm talking about for the here and now."

"Deal," she said immediately.

NOBODY WAS MORE pleasantly surprised than him when this agreement between the two of them not only ended up with them actually following through and checking in with each other regularly every week and sometimes every couple days but also to find their relationship deepening and broadening in some ways. Only as he understood how much she needed his participation in this did he realized how much he also needed hers.

They weren't lifelines reaching for each other, not realizing what they needed until they found it. They were both on floatation devices, doing their darnedest to stay up there, surviving—and just knowing that they weren't alone in that massive agony kept them floating and moving toward their goals.

It was a surprise when, at the end of one of his sessions, Dr. Garrick, the psychologist, looked at Heath in shock and said, "I see a great deal of progress," she said. "Do you care to share how and why?"

Heath gave a laugh. "Amid all these patients here, and the staff so eager to help, I finally stepped out and connected with somebody who's also going through a tough time." At that, the psychologist frowned. Heath shook his head. "No frowns, Doctor. It's not too much. It's not dark. It's not light. It's just … reality."

"Care to share with whom?"

"No," Heath said. "Just know that I'm in a happier place right now, and I think it's because of this person." He was careful to withhold Hailee's gender in case that raised all kinds of flags with the doctor too.

He could see that the doctor remained a little worried, almost felt like the doctor believed this should be questioned. Yet, at the same time, progress was progress.

"It's fine," Heath said quietly. "I, at least, am seeing a pathway forward."

The doctor made a decisive nod at that. "And we're definitely happy to see that. I just want to make sure that you're not getting into something that'll cause you more trouble later."

"I don't think so."

"Good. In that case, we'll check in with you in a couple days. How's that?"

"Make it next week maybe," he said.

"I can do that," she said. They set up the next time.

When he got up and grabbed his crutches, she said, "You're also moving easier."

"I am," he said. "Lots of things in my world are feeling easier right now."

"Good," she said. "Now if only you were sleeping better. I look forward to seeing your progress on that next week then too."

He used his crutches to get to the door, where he stopped, turned to the doc, and said, "It really does feel better from this new position."

She looked up at him in surprise, nodded, and said, "And that's excellent news. The fact that you can even see yourself in a different place from where you were is enormous progress."

"And I know exactly who to thank for that," he said with a chuckle.

"Make sure you thank them," the doctor said. "Sometimes people don't realize how much of a benefit they are because nobody takes the time to tell them."

He cocked his head to the side, looked at her, and nodded. "That's a good point," he said. "Maybe I'll do just that." And he headed out, wondering if he could find where Hailee was right now while he remembered. He made his way down the hallway and up to the front to the offices. He stopped at the front desk where Caitlin was and asked, "Any idea where Hailee is?"

"I think she's in her office," she said, "but she has a meeting with somebody right now."

He nodded, looked over at the door he thought was hers, then uncertain, asked, "Is that hers?"

Caitlin smiled and nodded. "Yes, she's the accountant."

At that, he was surprised that they'd never discussed what she actually did at this place, and he was glad that she had a professional job that would at least help her to make her way in the world. He leaned back against the wall and realized that, just because he couldn't hear the words through the door, the voices were coming out, though muffled, distorted. He didn't want to listen in, but, at the same time, something important here tugged at him, something that he needed to figure out. He wasn't sure what it was, but it was bugging him.

Finally he gripped his crutches and headed down the hallway. As much as he wanted to see Hailee, he needed to figure this out first. There was something familiar, yet something odd that he was getting. But what was it? As he hobbled back to his room and entered his doorway, it continued to puzzle him, but he couldn't place it. And it would bug him until he figured it out.

Hailee's voice sounded similar to the cleaning lady's, just … not quite the same.

# Chapter 13

I T WAS AMAZING how quickly Hailee had adjusted to her new schedule as an accountant, but she was worried about Heath. She hadn't told him that she was the cleaning lady and neither had she told him that she knew he was still struggling to sleep. When she saw him next, it was a few days after their weekly check-in. She had a cup of coffee in her hand and saw him sitting out in the deck, soaking up the sun. She detoured to head toward him, finding that she was craving a few minutes of their connection. It was a dangerous path for her, given that she didn't want to enter into any kind of relationship at this point in time, but he was a friend and solace, a place to rest her weary soul every once in a while. And she was starting to feel more for him than she was ready to admit.

As she came upon him, she asked, "You're not sleeping still?"

He opened his eyes slowly and looked up at her, then smiled. "Some days are better than others."

She frowned and nodded. Inside, she vowed to find a solution. It was the least she could do.

He looked at her coffee and said, "Is this a break for you?"

She nodded. "As much as I take a break, yes. I would have made it back to my office, but then I saw you sitting here."

He smiled. "Got a moment?"

"Of course," she said. She pulled out a chair and sat down. "The sun is hot," she exclaimed in surprise.

"I didn't notice," he said.

"Not too many people can handle the Texas heat all the time," she murmured.

"I was raised in Houston," he said, then opened his eyes and looked back at her. "Not that I have any family left, of course."

"Interesting you came back here," she said. "And that you didn't want a complete change."

"A change I wasn't really ready for," he said. "I think I was still trying to make connections to forge parts of my life into some semblance of a new reality that still contains some of the old as I continue forward."

She understood what he meant. When your foundation was ripped apart, like his had been, you grasp at straws to try to weave them together into a lifeline of something you know, something you can live with, something that you can move forward with. Because she'd done the same thing. That's why she was still here. Part of her wanted to run away and go to the opposite side of the country, and the other part of her couldn't leave everything she'd known.

And yet, she also knew it wasn't terribly healthy to sit here and spend all her time thinking about her child, thinking about her lost marriage, and thinking about all they could have been together. Instead she plunked down her butt and straightened her shoulders and dealt with the debt that she'd been left with. Speaking of which, she still hadn't heard from her lawyer. She frowned, making a mental note to contact him when she went back to her office.

"That looks like you just remembered something unpleasant."

"I did," she said. "I have to contact my lawyer."

"Sometimes I wonder if a lawyer is of any value when you spend as much money securing their services as you might have lost without them."

"I've thought about that a couple times," she said. "In this case, he's doing this pro bono."

"Wow," he said. "I'm happy for you."

"This lawyer spends his time dealing with the medical bills that some people are enslaved with for life," she said. "I just happened to luck into him and have him helping me to figure out how to reduce mine. It's pretty overwhelming."

"Well, let's hope he can help you," Heath said quietly. "I get that we're supposed to pay for services and for the treatments given, but sometimes it looks like the costs are incredibly overpriced."

"Like ten dollars for one aspirin. And there's no justification for it," she said. "You get this long list and this horrific dollar figure at the bottom of the page, and it just makes no sense at all."

"Well, if it's good news, hopefully you'll share it with me."

"I will," she promised. "I just don't know how long it'll be until I get any good news."

He nodded. "I think I heard about a couple charities that helped people retire medical debt too."

"That would be an interesting option," she said, looking at him in surprise. "It's certainly something that, unless you're caught up in this nightmare, you don't understand the magnitude of these bills. And then, when it is something that happens to you, it just becomes crushing."

"And your husband?"

She gave him a flat stare. "He skated. Then I was let go of my job. Lost my health benefits."

He nodded grimly. "You haven't had an easy time of it, have you?"

She nodded and said, "Nope, I haven't. But, like you, I'm dealing." She pushed her chair back. "And now I had to return to work."

"Just don't forget to contact the lawyer," he said. "One of these days, you've got to catch a break."

"One of these days I will," she said. She gave him a small wave and headed off. But, in the back of her mind, it was hard to imagine any kind of break that would help her. With her luck, her "break" would more likely be a broken leg from falling down the stairs or something equally stupid. Although she worked and lived in a medical facility, she wasn't so sure she'd get that kind of treatment here. And how sad that she now had full medical and dental at a point in time when she didn't need it, not with her new salary. And yet, when she did need it, she'd lost it all. She shook her head, desperately trying to keep the depression from overwhelming her yet again.

When she returned to her office, she sat down and brought up her email, then typed out a note to her lawyer, asking if there'd been any progress. She also asked as to whether anything could be done about the former employer and whether there were charities that helped to chip away medical debt that she could access. She put a note at the bottom, saying, *I know I'm obviously way too hopeful, but, if anything else could take this monkey off my back or at least help me bear that cost to be paid, it would be helpful.*

She quickly sent it before she gave herself a chance to

rethink it. And, with that done, she returned her attention to the day's work.

HEATH WATCHED HER go, shifting in his chair to see her walk away. He'd wanted to ask her if she was the cleaning lady, but it had seemed so very wrong, and, after having heard her voice in person just now, he'd immediately begun doubting himself. And, even if she was the former cleaning lady, so what? Was he supposed to ask her to go back to mopping the damn floors at two in the morning? That obviously wasn't an answer.

Even if she did need a second job, she could do much better than a cleaning lady for wages. But then maybe he was wrong. Perhaps cleaning ladies made a lot more money than Heath thought. It was just all so damn sad. And the last thing he wanted was to lose their relationship. If he were honest, he'd been interested in seeing their relationship develop further. It was nice to have Hailee here as a connection, somebody he looked forward to seeing.

When he shifted back around, Stan stood there, his hands on his hips, staring at him with a big grin on his face. Heath had finally met Stan a few weeks earlier but hadn't had a whole lot to do with the vet, but he was looking forward to more time with the animals. "What's that look for?" he asked with a half smile of his own.

"Do you think you can make it downstairs?" Stan asked.

Heath's eyebrows shot up. "Well, I can, even without an elevator, but why?" he asked cautiously.

"Because I have some unusual guests downstairs," he said. "I'm bringing some of the guys down one or two at a time to come meet them."

"I'm game," he said. "I was down there once, but it seemed like so much chaos that I didn't want to add to it. I left." He slowly straightened, using his crutches.

Stan looked at Heath's crutches, then looked at him, and said, "Let's take the elevator." And together, the two of them headed downstairs. Once inside Stan punched the button down to his place.

"Why me?"

"Why not you?" Stan asked. "I wanted to bring Hailee too. I saw the two of you talking, but she got up and left before I had a chance to invite her."

"I think she feels like she can't come down because she's working."

"Probably," Stan said. "I'll send her a message in a little bit."

"Okay," he said, mystified and wondering how he'd been the one invited. He rested on his crutches until the door opened, and he slowly made his way out. The elevator hallway was off to the side. They had to go through big double doors to get into the vet clinic. Once in there, he was surprised to find it mostly empty. "Not very busy these days?"

"Everybody is in the back," he said, and he opened up another set of double doors and led Heath into what looked like a large treatment room. Dani stood in the middle, her arms full of something big and wholly furry and fuzzy.

Heath stared at it and asked, "What is it?"

Dani smiled, walked closer, and a huge paw came out and batted him in the face.

"They're bobcats," Stan said. "This is Mama, and she has two kittens here too."

Dani added, "She has been at a local zoo. It's more of a rescue, but the cats hadn't been checked over, and her claws were causing some trouble. So all three have come in for Stan to take a look at them." The bobcat in Dani's arms wiggled, twisting almost like a smooth silken bundle and reaching for Heath.

With his crutches, it was hard for him to hold the big cat. He immediately sat down, and Dani shifted the huge feline onto his lap. Instantly a massive engine kicked in, and she rubbed her head against his. But it was more of a head-butt than a rub.

Dani quickly caught his crutches threatening to fall, which would cause chaos with the cats by the sudden noise. She put them to the side against the wall.

Heath's arms wrapped around the massive cat as its tongue came out and snaked once across his neck, like sandpaper swiping against his skin. He laughed and reached up to scratch the mama cat's ears. "Wow," he said. He turned to look at Dani, but she now had a much smaller version of his.

She sat down beside him and said, "You don't get to see these guys very often."

"You're not kidding," he said. He was amazed at the power and intelligence in its gaze. "She is beautiful."

Dani nodded. "These guys are fixed, and so is Mom. But like, wow. I love it when Stan gets to deal with animals other than the normal dogs and cats."

"Are you down here often?" Heath asked hesitantly.

"Every chance I get," Dani said. "It's either here or out in the pastures with the horses."

Stan stood behind them, checking the paw of the other bobcat kitten, and, when he was satisfied, he handed off the kitten to another man standing here. He had one leg in an odd-looking prosthetic at the end. He immediately sat down to cuddle the kitten.

"This is a huge advantage to being here," Heath said. The big feline tried to settle into his lap and, using Heath's chest and shoulders, hooked her claws in. Even as he gasped in pain, he smiled because the feline immediately draped across his arm. "What does she weigh? Thirty, forty, fifty pounds?" He gasped.

"If she's too much for you ..." Dani said, immediately standing up.

He shook his head. "No, not at all," he said. "I was just amazed at the size of her." Only then Stan came over and had some kind of a treat in his hand. He held it out for the big cat in Heath's arms, and she immediately snagged it up with one of her paws. She sniffed it carefully and then ate it with complete aplomb.

"She's so tame," he said.

"Yes, and no," Stan said. "Tame in the sense that she's well used to being handled, but that doesn't mean, if a rabbit or something went across the front yard, she wouldn't go after it in two seconds."

"Right," he said. "That makes a whole lot of sense." He stared at her, mesmerized. "She's still beautiful." He held her for another few minutes, until she got bored and started looking around for something else. She slid off his legs and stalked something that only she appeared to see as she headed toward the doorway.

Stan called out, "Let's make sure she doesn't go out that door."

"I hear you," Dani said. She turned to the man holding the kitten. "George, are you taking these guys back now?"

He nodded. "Yeah, now that they're all checked over. I'll get them loaded back up again."

Heath realized that the big female had a harness on. He didn't even notice that earlier. "Does she walk on a leash?"

"No, not well," George said with a half grin. "I have a cage for these two babies to move them, and I have converted the back of my truck into a complete cage. I'll just move Mama up into that and take her back."

"She appears to like field trips just fine," Heath said. He stood and watched while a leash was clipped onto the back of the big female's chest harness. Then he smiled and asked, "Her name is?"

"Rascal," George said with a smile. "I thought she was male at first, and then, all of a sudden, we've got two kittens."

At that, Heath chuckled out loud. "Well, that's a pretty rascally move on her part."

"It sure is," he said. With the kittens moved into their big carrying crate, a typical crate that any dog or cat would have been put into, Stan picked up the container, and they moved all three of the animals outside. Heath sat back down again at a spot where he could watch them load up the family of bobcats into the truck.

Dani stood at his shoulder.

"That's pretty special," he admitted.

"Absolutely," she said.

Just then another cat, a huge black cat—missing one ear and his tail looked to have been hacked off somewhere along the halfway mark—hopped up on its back legs, putting its front paws on Heath's knees and just glared. Heath looked at him for a long moment and said, "Okay. So the look in this guy's eyes is not terribly friendly."

Dani smiled, reached down, and scratched the battered cat between the eyes. "He's amiable, but he's probably pissed off at you because you gave the bobcats time and attention, but you have yet to greet him."

Hesitantly Heath reached out a hand and gently chucked the black cat under the chin.

Almost immediately the cat's eyes closed, and he leaned in. "So, does he always look like he's ready to tear a strip off you?"

"That's about right. He's a rescue, and, as you can see, he has suffered a little bit."

"I can see that," he said. "Still, he's beautiful too." At that, the cat immediately took advantage and jumped into Heath's lap, then settled in with his eyes closed. "Is he falling asleep now?"

Stan walked over and took one look. "Well, at least he found you."

"What's his name?"

"Mystique," he said.

"I think Mystique and Rascal should have their names switched," he said.

"I do too," Stan said. But he shrugged. "The thing is, this cat responds to the nickname *Misty*." When he said his name sharply, the cat immediately spun his head back and around and looked at him.

Heath just chuckled. "Is he a permanent resident too?"

"We're trying to adopt him out," Stan said, picking up the great big black cat from Heath's arms, while Stan urged them all back inside. Stan carried Misty to the counter, put him down, and gave him two treats. Mystique sprawled out flat to eat them. "But he was returned because he didn't settle in well."

"Why not?" Heath asked, as he dropped into a waiting room chair, hanging onto his crutches.

"Honestly I think he missed us," Stan said. "He does get a fair bit of attention here."

"I've seen Helga, Chickie and a couple other animals, but I've never seen this guy."

"Well, now that you've met him," Dani said, "he'll find your room."

"Seriously?"

"Oh, yeah, absolutely. It's almost like, if you don't make his acquaintance, he won't make yours. But, once he knows you, he'll be all over you."

"Well, he's welcome in my room anytime," Heath said. He grabbed the chair for support and slowly stood, then positioned his crutches under his armpits, smiled at the other two, and said, "Thank you. You don't realize just how much you miss animals until you come down here and get a moment to be with them."

"You can come back anytime you want," Stan said. "And, of course, we've always got the animals outside looking for some love too."

"Animals beyond the horses and the llama?"

"And the dogs that wander around."

As soon as he made it to the elevator, Heath headed upstairs. Stan was supposed to contact Hailee about the bobcats, but they were gone already. Still, Heath wouldn't let an opportunity like that pass by without talking to her. She was his go-to person, his go-to friend. She was quickly becoming something else in his mind. He just had to reconcile who he was now with who he'd been, and he knew that she had her own hurdles to relationships as well. In both cases, it was likely all about trust.

He didn't trust himself, and she didn't trust anyone else.

He shook his head and changed his mind from going to her office, choosing instead to head back to his own room. He didn't want to think too much, but sometimes he just needed space and time alone. As he headed there, he met up with Shane.

Shane looked at him for a long moment. "We didn't have a workout today. Have you been in the pool?"

"No," he said a little belligerently. "All I really wanted was some time alone."

Shane nodded, as if picking up on his tone. "You can't go more than two days without something. You understand that, right?"

"We had PT yesterday," he said in relief as he walked past. "I just needed some downtime today."

"So you just come up from being outside?"

At that, he stopped and smiled at Shane. "Yes, and no, I was holding a bobcat in my arms. Stan had a female and two kittens in."

Shane's face fell. "That's not fair. I'd have been down there if I had known."

"Well, maybe I was just lucky today. I was sitting on the deck when Stan came up to tell me that I needed to come down and take a look at the animals he had."

"You're lucky," Shane said. "Stan is a special guy. He understands animals, and he *says* that he doesn't understand humans, but I think he's wrong. It seems like he understands people more than we expect. You know that you can go down there any time, right? And put your name on a list if they need help?"

"I didn't know," Heath said. "Maybe I'll do that. It was great to have some exposure to the animals."

"It looks like you brought a friend with you," Shane said with a chuckle and pointed behind him.

Awkwardly Heath turned, using the crutches to keep his balance, to see Mystique, the big black male, racing behind him. And, sure enough, he stopped right at Heath's feet, then looked up at him, and meowed.

"Wow," Heath said as he struggled to bend down and give him a scratch. "Last I saw him, he was downstairs in the vet's waiting room."

"He's a bit of a survivor, this guy," Shane said, as he too reached down and scratched Mystique. "Are you heading back to your place now?"

"Yeah," he said. "I was just looking for some time-out." He shrugged. "I know that seems odd, but I'm still adjusting to being with people all the time."

"It can take a bit to adjust." Shane nodded. "But what you don't want to do is step out so long and so hard because, by then, it'll be challenging to get back into being with people."

"Sounds like my last year," Heath admitted.

"Well then, why don't you join up with one of the guys playing pool or one of the board games going on? Dinner is not for another hour so."

"Maybe," Heath said, but he hesitated.

"Or go for that swim," Shane said. "As soon as you start to slide deeper into that black hole, it's important to remember that even a walk around will kick in some endorphins and make things not quite so bad."

"If I could get some sleep," Heath said, "it wouldn't be so bad at all." And, with that, he headed back to his room, Mystique tagging along.

# Chapter 14

A COUPLE DAYS later Hailee once again came across Heath. This time he had collapsed on one of the large couches in a common area, looking morose and upset. She stepped in front of him. "You look like you could use a friend," she said quietly.

He looked up at her. "I need sleep. I just can't seem to sleep past two o'clock in the morning."

She frowned. She felt guilty that she had in effect abandoned him when she gave up her cleaning lady job to be Dani's accountant. Obviously he needed her back as the cleaning lady again. "How about white noise, instrumental music, or meditation?"

"It seems like I've tried it all," he growled. He gave an irritated shrug and then struggled to his feet. "I've got to go to PT." And crutched away from her.

She stood in the middle of the room with a frown, watching him as he left.

When he got to the where the room morphed into the hallway, he turned, looked back, sighed, and said, "I didn't mean to snap at you."

Her eyes were gentle. "Of course not. I understand."

"I know," he said. "And it's almost as bad."

"How do you figure?"

"Because I don't want you to have to understand. I just

would like to be healthy so that nobody has to go out of their way to actually understand what's going on in my world." Then he waved a hand. "I don't even know what I'm saying."

"No, but maybe I do," she said quietly. She walked toward him. "You want to be normal, so nobody has to go out of the way or make any extra effort."

He nodded. "Something like that. But this lack of sleep ..."

"Nightmares still?"

"Yeah," he said. "It's always the nightmare of the crash. They just never seemed to go away. I had a method before of getting back to sleep, but it looks like nothing works anymore."

She frowned as he stormed off on his crutches. When she walked back toward her office, she stopped in at Dani's office and said, "He's still not sleeping."

Dani, preoccupied, looked up, but obviously confusion was in her gaze. "Who's not sleeping?"

"Heath."

Dani nodded, comprehension filling her gaze. "No, he isn't. It's a definite problem."

Hailee stood in the doorway for a long moment. "Meditation? White noise? Music? Have any of those things helped?

"No, not at all." Dani looked at her in surprise. "Good thought though."

Hailee looked out over the window not sure what to say. Except...

"I'll talk to his team and see if there is anything else we might try." Dani frowned down at her desk as if already wondering who to contact.

"I know," Hailee said. She took a deep breath and added, "On a side note, I was wondering if you needed another cleaning lady. I could do a few hours in the evening.".."

"No," Dani said firmly. "One job for you. You are making enough now you don't need to do that."

"Hey, maybe he was falling asleep to my mopping," she joked. "We could try it," Hailee said slowly, "if it worked, maybe we'd find another way to make that work out for him permanently?"

"You mean, like having my current cleaning lady come by at that hour? Because you certainly aren't going back to that." Dani looked at her pencil, tapping her desktop.

"Well, that's possible," Hailee said. "But it doesn't mean her mop strokes will have the same rhythm, and we can hardly teach or expect another cleaning lady to maintain my particular rhythm so somebody else can sleep."

"I'm glad you said that," Dani said gently, "because that is an imposition."

"It might be worth a try." Hailee didn't know what else to do or say so quietly withdrew. But she couldn't let go of it as she went through the rest of her day and evening. She did go to bed at ten, but she set her alarm for two. As soon as she woke up, she quickly dressed and headed to the central part of the building.

There, she went into the utility closet and pulled out her mop. She filled her bucket with hot water because, if she was out here and she would be mopping, then she might as well do an excellent job of it. When she passed one of the other cleaning ladies, the woman just ignored her. And that was the way Hailee wanted it. She went two doors down Heath's hallway and proceeded to slowly and methodically mop the floor.

Coming back up against Heath's door, she spent a few extra minutes there, slowly mopping. She didn't know if he was awake or asleep or if she was making any difference tonight, but she kept up the rhythm as she had done before for him. By the time the hallway was done, it was well past three.

She emptied out her mop bucket and put all her equipment away, then went back to bed. The next morning, she got up, tired, yawning in the middle of her coffee, as she headed to her office. By then, she needed food so went for a coffee break and grabbed an apple. She walked out on the deck, lifting her face to the sun. A few minutes later, she heard a voice behind her. She turned, saw Heath, and smiled. "Wow," she said. "Don't you look better."

He nodded. "Maybe I finally turned the corner. For some reason last night I slept really well."

"Did you wake up?" She didn't know how to take the news. Great that he slept, but she was so tired that it's obvious she couldn't do this every night.

He frowned, searched her face, then shrugged. "I might have, but I fell back asleep again. I know I'll need lots more sleep like this, but, man, that really made a huge difference."

She smiled. "I hear you. Nothing like getting a good night's sleep."

As she headed back to her office, she felt good. She didn't know if it was from her own mopping, but the fact was, he'd had a good night's sleep, and she herself identified with just how valuable that was for healing. She didn't know if she should even try to keep it up, but she thought, if she did it for a couple nights and then didn't do it, maybe she could tell if Heath was sleeping better because of her mopping. She felt foolish getting up every night doing this, but she was determined to try and see him through it. Nothing in the world helped a soul heal as much as the proper rest.

She went through that new routine for the next three nights. Getting up and mopping his floor, putting away everything, not saying a word to anyone, and then falling back into bed. On the fourth night, she didn't do it. And, when she got up Friday morning, she'd slept better because she hadn't gotten up in the night, but now she was racked with guilt.

Instead of going to the cafeteria first, she headed to her office and started in on her work. She didn't hear from anybody and, of course, why would anybody know about her experiment, much less be worried about it? But finally she had to find out, and it was lunchtime. It was early, so she got up and headed to the cafeteria, looking for him. She saw no sign of him. She looked around, and then, after she'd eaten, she grabbed a coffee and a muffin to take back to her office and headed by his room. He was coming out as she went past. She stopped, smiled at him, and said, "Hey."

He nodded and said, "Hey."

But it was apparent he wasn't too happy. She frowned. "Not a good night?"

He shrugged. "I guess I can't have good nights every night. I did for the last several nights, and I thought maybe I had turned the corner, but last night was one of those rude awakenings that I really didn't need."

"Aah," she said, "I'm sorry." Inside, her heart sank. She felt guilty but gave him a warm smile and said, "Maybe you'll have another good night tonight."

"Maybe," he said, but he didn't look at all convinced.

She walked away, feeling terrible, because there had to

be a start and stop to this, and she just didn't know what to do about it. She quickly turned and headed back to her office. As a test, it was minor and inconclusive, but it was definitely leaning toward the fact that maybe she had been the reason that he had been sleeping. And that made her feel even worse for not following up with it.

Surely she could do something for him. But, for the rest of the day and that evening, she determined she would return and do the mopping. And it was two o'clock when she headed back up again. This time, when she walked into the hallway, Dani stood there, her arms crossed over her chest, frowning at her.

Feeling guilty, but not knowing what else to do but to continue with her plan, she held up a finger to Dani and slowly and methodically mopped the floor. When she was done, Dani standing there and watching her in amazement, Hailee gathered up her bucket and grabbed her mop and pointed to the far end of the hallway.

Once they walked there, Dani asked in a low voice, "Why?"

Together, the two of them walked through the silent building and back out to the big deck, where usually Hailee would go downstairs to her own apartment. There, with the two of them under the moonlight, Hailee explained about Heath not sleeping without the mopping sound. Dani looked at her in surprise. "Well, I knew that he was looking for the cleaning lady from weeks ago," she said. "I hadn't realized it was connected to his sleep pattern."

Hailee nodded. "And I only started again a few days ago. He just looked so ragged all the time, and I thought that, if I could at least help him get a good night's sleep, he would heal."

Dani's small smile started at the corner of her lips, and, before long, her whole face held a big beautiful smile. "You really care about him, don't you?"

"I shouldn't," Hailee said hurriedly. "It's terrible to care."

"No," Dani said, immediately reaching out a hand to squeeze Hailee's fingers. "It means being human."

"But it hurts," Hailee said in a low voice. "It hurts so damn much."

The two women stared off in the distance. "The thing is, words can say a lot," Dani said, "but they don't show the person on the inside. So then, when you listened to the words, but you didn't actually see who was under them—when their actions and their words didn't match—you felt abandoned and bereft. Yet now, in your case, you didn't tell anybody what you were doing, but your efforts were there because all you were trying to do was give Heath a good night's sleep. Do you know how few people would get up in the middle of the night to come mop the floor outside his room so that he could sleep?"

"You know how many people would think I was nuts for doing it?" Hailee said, a small smile playing at the corner of her mouth. "Or how crazy he is for needing that?"

"It doesn't matter as to the wisdom of it or whether anyone understands it," Dani said. "After we've seen as many patients as we have, we realize that we're all unique, and, for whatever reason, that sound cemented something for him, and it allowed him to fall back asleep. And, when he lost it, and I didn't realize it was that severe, he couldn't rest anymore. Shane said that he'd taken a couple steps back, but I hadn't really understood why."

"Well, the real trick," Hailee said, "is if Shane says this

last week that Heath has improved because I've been doing this for the week. Then I stopped last night, and Heath had a terrible night, so I returned tonight so he could sleep again."

"Wow," Dani said. "That's devotion."

Hailee stopped and frowned because, in some ways, she didn't even think about it and, indeed, hadn't labeled it. "I don't really want to think of it that way," she muttered.

"Too bad," Dani said, "because you do not see your actions for what they are."

"Why?" she said defiantly. "I'm just trying to be nice."

But Dani's eyes saw a whole lot more. "Are you telling me that your heart doesn't flutter when you get close to him? That you don't spend a good part of your day wondering if you can detour so you can pass his room or meet up with him in the cafeteria? And that you don't look forward to the meetings that you have planned with him?"

"All of that just means we're good friends," Hailee said. "Or that we're heading toward being good friends."

Dani's smile was luminous in the darkness. "Oh, it does, indeed," she whispered. "But it also says so much more. There's a connection between the two of you. And, if you're lucky, it'll become something so much more."

"But then I have to trust," Hailee whispered back. "And I lost so much last time."

"You lost everything important," Dani said with a nod. "But that doesn't mean it will happen a second time, and it doesn't mean that it wasn't worth going down that path in the first place. Do you regret having Jacob in your life?"

Hailee looked at her in horror. "Of course not. He was everything to me."

"So, when you lost him," she said quietly, "you lost everything important. But, if you hadn't gone down that path, if you hadn't tried, you wouldn't have had him in your life in the first place. So I'd like to believe that everything happens for a reason. And, even though your husband turned out to be a waste of human space and absconded before he had to deal with the pain of losing his own child, that just makes him a weak person with a whole lot more lessons to learn.

"And I'd rather see you fall back in love again, even if it hurts a second time because through that hurt we grow. And through that hurt, great things come, like Jacob. Yes, Jacob wasn't on this earth for long, and it hurt you tremendously to lose him. But just imagine how empty you would be inside if he hadn't even shown up in the first place?" With that, she patted Hailee gently on the shoulder and gave her a quick hug. "Now that I know what you're up to in the middle of the night, I'm going to bed."

As she walked away, Hailee turned and called out, "How did you know I would be there?"

"The other cleaning lady," she said. "She asked why I was hiring somebody to do just that hallway and what was she not doing good enough."

Hailee laughed. "She's doing a good job," she said. "She just wasn't doing it at the right time or with the right rhythm."

Dani smiled and nodded. "So I came to see for myself, ... and this isn't over by the way." She shook a finger at her. "We do need a better solution than this."

"Well, it'd be nice to get my own sleep," Hailee said.

"Absolutely," Dani said. "And that's something you have to consider."

"Maybe," Hailee said, "but I still don't want him to end up with no sleep."

"I hear you, but that's not always the same thing."

"No, it isn't, and that's why we have to sort through this."

"Maybe we can," Dani said. "I'll see what I can do."

And, with that, Hailee headed to bed herself.

THE NEXT MORNING Heath woke up, feeling rested and relaxed. He rolled over slowly, feeling a sense of inner peace in his life. "Finally," he muttered. "I was so afraid those few nights would just be the oddity, and I'd never sleep again." When a hard knock came on his door, he called out, "Come in." He watched in surprise as Shane headed in.

Shane saw him in bed, stopped, and said, "Wow, does that mean you had a good night or a bad night?"

"A good night again," Heath said, slowly shifting in the bed, so he was leaning against the headboard. "I literally just woke up a few minutes ago. I gather I'm late?"

"Not necessarily," Shane said. "I can push you back a bit if you want."

"Well, coffee and some food would probably be a good idea." At that, his tummy rumbled.

Shane smiled. "Well, absolutely nothing is better for you than a good night's sleep, so the chances are that we'll just push this back to this afternoon, if you've got time. Maybe we'll do a pool session instead."

"Perfect. The pool sounds great. What time is it?"

Shane, heading back to the hallway already, turned and laughed at him. "It's past ten-thirty." And he was gone.

Heath stretched out in the bed. "Is that what good sleep's all about?" He slowly sat up and stretched again. Even though he was stiff, and some parts of him were sore, the rest of him felt so damn good that it was almost impossible to sort it out. He tried to remember whether he'd woken up in the night and thought he'd surfaced once or twice and then had fallen under again.

Maybe he wasn't thinking about his cleaning lady anymore. Perhaps he was finally past that hurdle. He got up, showered, dressed, and, by the time he made it into the cafeteria, he was already heading for the lunchtime crowd. Dennis took one look at him and said, "Wow, you look bright-eyed and cheerful."

"I slept solid and slept late too," he said. "Now I'm starving."

Dennis immediately loaded him up with fried chicken and a big plate of greens. "Here you go."

He crutched to an empty table on the deck and sat down out in the sunshine. He sat here for a long moment, sipping his coffee and looking around him. When Dani happened upon him a few moments later, he looked up, smiled, and said, "Quite the place you got here, Dani."

She stopped, looking at him in surprise, and said, "Don't you look good today."

He raised an eyebrow. "You're like the third person to tell me that. I didn't realize just what a good night's sleep was doing for me."

"Last night?"

He nodded. "All of a sudden, I started to sleep again."

A small smile played at the corner of her lips. "Perfect," she said. "There's nothing better for you." And, with that, she disappeared. He saw her talking to Shane down at the far end, but he ignored them. He was totally okay to go to the pool this afternoon and to work out there, but he wanted food first. He attacked his lunch with gusto, and, by the time he made his way to the pool at two o'clock for his afternoon physical therapy session, Shane was there, waiting for him.

"Let's see what a good night's sleep has done for you," he said, and he proceeded to put him through the paces. By the time he was done, it was almost four-thirty, and Heath was in the hot tub.

"I think I did much better today," he said, staring up at the sky.

"There's no *think* about it," Shane said. "Now just repeat whatever that magical moment was that gave you all that sleep again."

He smiled and said, "I wish I knew."

As he went to bed that night though, he thought about it and wondered if he was still waking up at two o'clock or maybe just the silence now was setting him back to sleep again. He drifted off to sleep quickly. And, when he woke up later, he checked his watch to find it was yet again two a.m. He sighed and settled in and realized he would probably not get in a good night's sleep this time. As he drifted into a half dose, he heard in the background the same mopping sounds. He smiled, feeling that same sense of comfort, and he closed his eyes and drifted yet again back under.

He didn't know who was out there, but he was grateful that somebody was back, mopping the floor, almost as if just for him.

# Chapter 15

WHEN HAILEE CAME into work the next morning, both Dani and Shane waited for her in the hallway. She frowned at them both. "What's up?" They just shook their heads and waited until she unlocked her door and stepped inside. "Okay, now you've got me worried," she half joked. "What have I done?"

Shane smiled said, "You haven't done anything except be a perfect human being."

"Why is that?"

"Because Heath is progressing beautifully," he said. "I understand you're the little bird that may have been out there mopping the hallway in the middle of the night." She winced at that and glared at Dani.

Dani shrugged and said, "You can't expect the world not to find out."

"Does Heath know?"

"No," Shane said. "But you should probably tell him."

"Why? It'll just make him feel guilty."

"How so?" Dani asked.

"He won't want his sleep at the cost of my sleep," she said bluntly.

"Maybe not," Shane said. "So we need a solution."

"Not sure what that is though," she said.

"Well, I have a suggestion," Dani said. "It might take a

little bit to make it work though. I don't want to say too much about it, in case I can't get it to come together. Let me think it through and get back to you."

Hailee nodded and settled in for the day. When she looked up, it was already eleven, and, sure enough, Heath was at her doorway with a bright smile on his face. "Hey," she said.

"Well, it looks like I'm doing well for sleeping, but you? I'm not so sure."

"Hey, I'm not sleeping too bad," she said with as bright a smile as she could muster.

"No," he said, "maybe not, but I can see you're not sleeping precisely the same as I am."

"Well, I don't think you were sleeping for a long time, so it's hardly a surprise that you're doing better now that you're finally getting some sleep."

He nodded. "Got time for lunch?"

"Sure, why not?" she said. And she looked at her desk, smiled, and said, "I just need a couple minutes to put stuff away."

"I'll head down because I'm slower than you," he said. "I'll see you there."

She smiled and locked up her office and headed in behind him. She caught up with him just as he went into the cafeteria. "Good timing," she said.

He smiled and stepped up to talk to Dennis. "I want all of it," he declared. Dennis burst out laughing but gave him a huge plateful. Hailee snagged it and carried both of their plates down the aisle.

Soon Heath and Hailee were both sitting outside. Not in the sun because it was too hot but off to the side in the shade. They'd both been working on their individual problems. At least she thought so.

"How are you doing these days?" she asked.

"The world is a better place when you have sleep," he said almost complacently. She immediately felt guilty for even considering not doing the mopping. He just nodded and looked at her and said, "But obviously you're not feeling the same way."

Dani's words were in her mind as Hailee thought about that. "I'm learning to let go a little bit more," she said quietly. "It's not easy though."

"Nothing worth doing ever is," he reminded her.

She smiled. "Isn't that the truth?"

"Will you avoid relationships for the rest of your life?"

"Of course not," she said, and then she stopped and thought about that. "That was a trick question too."

"Not at all, but I figured it was probably more comfortable to ask you that one outright instead of beating around the bush."

"Do you even know my history?" She appreciated his honesty, even as she worried what he'd say if he knew it all.

"Some of it, yes," he said. "The rest? ... Well, it isn't too hard to connect the dots."

She quickly filled him in about Jacob's painful fight for life, right from day one, followed by the pain and the sense of betrayal she'd gone through with her husband, and the final straw—Jacob's death.

Heath listened quietly and sadly. "And, of course, it's no wonder why you don't want to trust anybody again."

"Maybe," she said with a half smile. "I might have been a little too quick to make that decision. Somebody reminded me that, if I hadn't met my husband, and if I hadn't married him, and if I hadn't had Jacob in the first place, there would have been this massive hole in my heart about a joy that I wouldn't even know that existed. So, even though it was painful, I would still have wanted Jacob in my life."

"Meaning that, even though you lost him, he was still such a joy that you're grateful he came to you in the first place."

"Exactly," she said. "And, therefore, I can't really begrudge my husband either."

"Are you divorced?"

"Yes," she said. "He divorced me. As soon as possible to get away from the situation."

"Well, maybe you'll be ready soon," he said.

"Maybe, but it would probably take somebody else in my life to make me care enough."

"Right." And, at that, he fell silent.

She looked up, realized that she, in a way, had cut him off from that and said, "And maybe it's time to do that." There was an odd silence, and she looked up to see him staring at her intently. She smiled at him and said, "I really enjoy the time we spend together."

"I'm glad," he said softly. "How have your nights been?"

"They've been great. I'm not sleeping as well as I could, but then I'm still dealing with stuff," she said with an airy wave of her hand.

"And how do you feel about being honest and open and not keeping secrets?"

"Sometimes secrets need to be kept," she said honestly. "If they'll hurt somebody to share them, I don't think they should be told." He just nodded and kept eating. She wondered where the question was going. "What about you?"

"It's like little white lies," he said. "I don't think there's any point in telling them if we don't have to, but sometimes telling a little white lie could save a world of hurt, yet it could cause a world of hurt in some instances. In the end, I don't really believe in hurting others unnecessarily."

She smiled at that. Because, of course, he didn't. "And are you dealing with your losses?"

"A little better than I expected," he said. "Now that I'm sleeping. Now that I've got an email." At that, he fell silent.

"What kind of an email?" she nudged.

"From the sister of one of my friends. It was an odd email, awkward, I guess. And I still haven't read it thoroughly."

"Maybe you should," she said.

"Maybe," he said, then shrugged. "But I read enough to realize that she doesn't blame me. Instead she thanked me for being in her brother's life. And that her brother, my best friend, had always spoken about me and how much he really loved spending time with me." At that, he seemed to choke up.

She reached across, gently laced her fingers with his, and said, "And I can see that. I'm thrilled she took the step to tell you that."

He nodded, smiled, squeezed her fingers, and then continued eating. "Me too."

HEATH HEADED BACK to his room after lunch, surprised that he'd even mentioned the email to Hailee. But, of course, she understood. So far, there hadn't been a whole lot that they hadn't had some level of understanding on. So, if she was the cleaning lady, why wouldn't she have said anything to him? Was it not important to her? And that just brought him back to being afraid that maybe he'd been wrong the whole time.

This time, he was determined to stay up and see who it was. He didn't want to put her on the spot, but, if it was her, well then, he didn't know what it meant. His heart raced when he thought about if it had been her, then what would it say? And, if it wasn't her, he had almost a deflated feeling to it. But also guilt and something he didn't want any more of. He couldn't turn off his mixed emotions for the rest of the day.

By the time he headed to bed that night, his whole mind-set was in turmoil. He hadn't seen her all afternoon, and then, at the end of the day, he'd seen her yawning. He frowned with that same need to sort it out, and he went back to his room and waited until the dinner hours were almost done before he headed in and got his.

He passed the evening answering emails and talking to his best friend's sister. She was married with two kids, and, as soon as he'd responded to her email, she phoned him. They'd spent a lovely hour talking and reminiscing about the men that had both been so special to them. When he hung up, he'd felt raw, heartsore, but also happy. And he realized that he'd reached yet another stage of grief and was actually capable of letting some of that guilt go. He headed to bed and, with a smile on his face, crashed right away.

When he woke up, it was once again two a.m. His body was into this weird rhythmical cycle that made no sense. He listened intently, but he couldn't hear the cleaning lady outside. He tossed and turned and then thought he heard something. He hesitated and listened intently. And there it was, that same rhythmical back-and-forth footsteps, with the rolling of the bucket and the swishing of the mop. He got out of bed, quietly grabbed his crutches, and crept forward until he stood right at the door. He could hear the cleaning lady's motions. He wondered, did he dare find out who it was. If it was some other lady, it might scare the crap out of her.

He leaned on his crutches and slowly and quietly opened the door to see who might be out there. He only opened it enough to stick his head out, and the hallway was dark. But there was a long, lean form, calmly and methodically mopping the floor. He couldn't tell for sure who it was. He wanted to see her face underneath the ambient light of the hallway. When she went around the corner, he would get just that second to find out. She yawned, then reached for the bucket and the mop, nudging them out of the way.

She turned, and his heart raced. It was her. Hailee. Ever-so-softly, he closed the door and thought about it. His heart raced with joy, but, at the same time, he knew it had to stop. He didn't know how or why she was doing this, but he could guess. It was one of the sweetest things he'd ever had done for him in his life.

He headed back to bed with a big smile on his face, and he fell asleep instantly.

# Chapter 16

S HE WAS YAWNING the next morning when she made it to her office. She put down her purse, turned on her computers, and then realized she couldn't do anything without coffee. She hadn't even had time for breakfast because she'd overslept. As she walked into the cafeteria, it was still full of people. She smiled and walked straight to the coffee, and Dennis called out, "Tut, tut, tut. You need more than coffee."

"You're a mother hen," she said to him.

"I am," he said. "I like to take care of all my chicks, and you're one of them. What would you like for breakfast? Something with more protein, like sausages and eggs, or something like yogurt and fresh fruit?"

"Yogurt and fresh fruit," she admitted, "with maybe a bit of granola?"

He pointed to several freshly made parfaits.

She nodded and said, "Is there one with seeds?"

"How about I make you one right now?" He grabbed an empty parfait glass and filled it in the layers that she requested. By the time he was done, he looked at it and said, "You know what? That looks mighty fine."

She smiled. "You're right."

She grabbed a spoon with the parfait glass on one hand and her coffee in the other, then headed back to the office.

As soon as she got inside, she sat and started eating. Dani called her extension and asked, "Hey, you got a moment?"

"Sure," she said. "I'm eating, but whatever."

"My office in ten minutes or so?"

"Perfect," she said. She sat back, checked her emails, finished her parfait, and tossed back the last of her coffee. Then she got up and headed to Dani's office. She greeted her friend with a bright smile, but Hailee's smile immediately fell off when she saw Shane and Heath here. She looked at them in surprise. "Sorry. Am I intruding?"

"Not at all," Dani said with a warm smile. "We're waiting for you. Close the door behind you, please."

Slowly closing the door, she took the last chair available and sat down. She wasn't sure her legs would support her at this point anyway. "What's up?"

"What's up?" Heath said, his voice was a little harsher than she'd ever heard from him. "I don't want you losing sleep to help me sleep."

She stared at him, wordlessly. "Sorry?"

"I saw you last night," he said. He shook his head. "You know I'm not exactly sure why you're doing what you're doing. If it's for the reason I think it is, then I really, really appreciate it, but I don't want to sleep if it means you don't get any."

"Uh," she said but then fell silent. She really didn't know what to say.

"*Uh?*" he repeated with an eyebrow raised.

She shrugged. "It's just, whenever I do mop the floors, you sleep. And when you were struggling so much for so many weeks without it, I realized how much it meant to you. And that I was being very selfish when it was something so simple that I could do to help." She didn't know why this conversation was happening in Dani's office, but both Dani's and Shane's attentions were going from Hailee to Heath, depending on who was speaking.

"I get that," he said, "and that's precisely why I thought you were doing it." And then he sighed heavily. "But you're also tired, and you're getting run-down. You're rising before two in the morning to come mop that hallway," he said in exasperation. "I wake up. I hear the mop, and I fall back asleep. Immediately. And I get that. But you were up earlier, getting dressed, coming up here, then spending an hour mopping that hallway. That's got to be the darnedest cleanest hallway in the entire place. And then I'm supposed to go back to sleep in just minutes, knowing that you've come up here, spent like ninety minutes of your own time in the middle of the night to mop so that I can sleep?" He shook his head. "I'll admit that I fell asleep last night with a smile on my face," he said, "but I don't want you doing it again."

She didn't even know what to say. She was ultimately embarrassed and felt extremely awkward. Not to mention hurt. "I hear you," she said. "And, of course, I won't if you don't want me to do." She tried to stand, moving the chair back out of the way.

Shane lifted a hand and said, "Stop."

She looked at him, refusing to look at Heath.

"He's not asking you to stop for the reason you think he is."

She frowned at Shane. "What other reason is there?" She used all of her experience of many years gone by. If life wasn't turning out the way she wanted it to, she'd put some steel in her spine. If she was getting a talking-to or things were turning out differently than she wished them to, well, that's fine. She'd face it and move on. She'd been here before.

"He doesn't want you to lose sleep because it makes him feel guiltier. And we're trying to stop the guilt."

Her mouth formed a small *O*. "I hadn't considered that."

"No, of course not," Heath said. "You were trying to do something beautiful for me, and it just makes me feel worse."

She frowned at him. "You could just take it as a gift that somebody wanted to give you," she said in a tart voice.

He grinned. "Well, I would. It's actually something I was talking to Dani and Shane about earlier," he said. "So I would ask you if maybe you could mop the floor once or twice again, perhaps more if we need to. And I know it's stupid, and I know that nobody else would even understand why the sound is putting me to sleep—except that I now remember my mother always did this in the evenings. After I went to bed, that's when she would clean.

"And I now recognize that that was the sound and the feeling of the comfort of home for me. It was the meaning of family. It was what I had before I lost so much. So, when you did that, it was like bringing back my childhood security blanket and wrapping it around me. And, for that, I am forever grateful because I think you've probably come up with the answer to how I can get over my insomnia."

She stared at him, a question in her gaze. "Okay. I guess that's a good thing?" she asked hesitantly. "I'm honestly still in the dark."

"I know," he said.

At that point, Dani stepped in. "We'll have you mop in the night again, when everything's quiet and soundless, and we'll record it. I do have some sound experts in town, and, once we've got the recording that we need, we'll give it to Heath as his own personalized white noise that he could use to go to sleep. Whether we give it to him as a CD or an MP3 format that he can play on his phone, I don't know yet. But we're hoping it will give him that same security-blanket feeling so he can sleep at night."

She sat down with a hard *thump*. "But that's wonderful," she said. "I didn't even think of that."

"Which is why we're all here in this room together right now," Shane said with a smile. "It's not that what you're doing was wrong. That's far from it. You actually solved a massive issue for us. We're just trying to find a way to make it happen without you losing your sleep too."

Hailee grinned. "Hey, as long as it works, I'm totally okay with doing this again."

HEATH HAD BEEN delighted with the solution. It had been something that they set up later without him even being aware of it because they wanted it to be as natural as they could. So several nights later he was presented with the MP3 player and with a CD and an MP3 file that he could play both on a small desk speaker system and also on his phone. So, at any time that he woke up in the middle of the night, he could just hit a button and hear the same sounds over and over again.

Now, four days later, with the first night under his belt with that recorded sound, he realized just what a blessing it was. Sometimes he wondered just how many memories he had left of his mother. He'd been young when she had died in a car accident, but he eventually remembered falling asleep to the sounds of her cleaning all the time.

And now here he was, once again falling asleep to sounds of somebody who cared enough about him to get up in the middle of the night to do that for him. He wanted to do something special for Hailee, but he wasn't exactly sure what. He'd sent out several emails, asking for more information, but, so far, there hadn't been too much response. He wanted a few moments of just some peace and quiet to talk to her about some options also and to let her know how he felt about her, more than just her mopping in the middle of the night to get him to sleep.

When he went to lunch, a look on his face must have relayed something because Dennis immediately asked in a low tone, "You okay?"

Heath looked up with a smile and said, "Yeah, I am. I was just thinking that maybe, instead of being in here, I'd find a way to get outside with the animals today."

"Well, why don't you have your main meal here," he said, "and I'll fix you a coffee and a couple cinnamon buns to-go, then you can take the elevator and go outside in the wheelchair or on your crutches and go to the horses?"

"That's not a bad idea," he said. "I need to touch base with the animals again."

"It sounds like you got woman troubles."

"Ha," he said. "Pretty hard to have woman troubles in here."

"Oh, I don't know," Dennis said. "I've watched a lot of couples form in this place. So, if it is, you just talk to old Dennis. I got a solution for you."

"Yeah, right," he said, and then he shook his head. "I'll eat lunch, and then I'll go down and spend some time thinking."

"Maybe you should do that," he said with a smile, and, sure enough, as soon as Heath finished eating, Dennis arrived with two big cinnamon buns and a cup of coffee in a thermos. "The buns are hot out of the oven," he said, as he then wrapped each of them in foil. "Take these with you, and maybe go visit with the animals," he said, putting the buns and a thermos in a reusable grocery bag. "Maybe over there where the llama is or someplace that you're comfortable."

Heath nodded. "That's a great idea." He slung the bag over his shoulder and slowly made his way downstairs and back outside on his crutches. He should have brought the wheelchair, but he preferred to do with the crutches as much as he could. He headed over to the long grass, and, rather than trying to get up onto the fence, he sat down against a post, his crutches beside him, wondering just what he was doing and where he was heading. When he heard a female voice call out to him a few minutes later, he looked over to see Hailee walking toward him, with a cup of coffee in her hand.

"Hey," she cried out, "may I join you?"

He smiled and said, "Absolutely."

She sat down beside him. "Ooh, cinnamon buns." She looked back up at the cafeteria and then shrugged and said, "It's too far to go."

"Well, I've got two," he said, "so how about you share with me?" And that's what they did, splitting up the cinnamon buns with an awkward, and yet peaceful silence between the two of them.

"So, how did it work?" she asked, studying his features.

He looked at her with a smile. "Perfect. You have no idea how grateful I am."

She shrugged. "Can't say gratitude is anything I particularly want," she said with a laugh. "But I'm glad it worked out."

"I understand," he said. Just then his phone beeped. He pulled it out and checked to see what the email was about and laughed. "On the other hand," he said, "I have something of a gift for you too."

"Really?" she said. "And what's that?"

He held out the email that was on this phone and said, "Read that."

She took his phone from him and slowly read it, her eyes widening as she stared at him in shock. He nodded and said, "I wasn't kidding when I said people are out there who work to help forgive medical debts."

"I actually heard from my lawyer, and the hospital has renegotiated my bill down by 75 percent," she whispered.

He looked at her in surprise and laughed. "Well, maybe between these two events, we can get you cleared of all your debts."

"And that," she said, "sounds too good to be true."

"Oh, I don't know," he said. "I think we often forget that good people are out there too."

She looked at the email again and said, "Is it for real?"

"They said so," he said. "They're offering $30,000 toward your medical debt."

"I don't have much more than that left to pay off," she said. "At least if what the lawyer says comes to pass."

"It probably will. We don't realize just how much of that medical debt is inflated. So, in this case, there's a good chance that you'll do just fine now."

"Wouldn't that be wonderful?" she said, laughing.

"And, if it is," he said, "what would you do with your

life now? Would you leave?"

She stared at him wide-eyed, then shook her head, and said, "No. I love it here. It's been the perfect place for me." Then she stopped and looked around. "How long are you here for?"

"Another month and a half, I think, maybe a little longer," he said. "And then I'll probably settle close by in Houston."

"Ah, good," she said.

Then more awkward silence came.

He finally took the bull by the horns and said, "And, even if I do move to Houston, I was hoping we'd be close enough to see each other. If your trust issues have come this far."

"Have your guilt issues?" she asked.

He nodded slowly. "I'm working on it, but having Wendy, Ben's sister, to talk to has really helped a lot."

She smiled and nodded. "You're right. And I've made some progress myself."

"Perfect," he said. His voice thickened. "So, do you think that's something you might be interested in?"

"What's that?"

He shook his head. "Let's not play games. I'm a straight shooter, and I think we've both had enough of the dishonesty in life to want to talk straight."

"If you're asking if I'm interested in seeing more of you? Absolutely," she said with a gentle smile. "But I was hoping we didn't have to wait until you went to Houston."

He looked at her and smiled. "Seriously?"

"I came out here to tell you about the email I got from the lawyer, and, as I was walking here, I realized that somehow you've become the friend I've never had," she said.

"Even when I was married, my husband wasn't somebody I could talk to like this. He wasn't somebody who I cared to share enough of my life with."

"So maybe you married the wrong person completely," he said with a smile.

She nodded and said, "It took me a long time to realize that I didn't do him a service either. And that I should have chosen somebody better for myself."

"So now what?" he asked.

"Well, I was kind of hoping," she said with a kink of her lips, "that maybe you'd be interested in the job."

"You mean, if I'd be interested in being a replacement?"

She shook her head immediately. "No, of course not."

"Good," he said, with a little more force than he intended. "Because I'm not a replacement for anybody. On the other hand," he said, "if you feel about me the way I do about you, I'd highly suggest that we entirely skip the whole talk of replacements and just start fresh and maybe create something unique between us."

She looked at him, then smiled, her eyes widening.

He leaned across and gently grasped her chin with two fingers, then tugged her closer. "At least if you feel the way I feel …" And he kissed her ever-so-gently.

Her lips curved under his, and she whispered, "I don't think you could possibly feel the way I feel about you because I think your heart would hurt too much."

"No," he said, "it's not about hurt. It's about being open enough to accept what's coming so that you're free and bright and happy."

"That sounds nice," she whispered. "I can definitely sign up for that."

And this time, when their lips met, it was a kiss of promise, and it was a kiss of hope. But, more than that, it was a kiss of growth for both of them, for a future neither had expected to find but was there waiting for them nonetheless.

# Epilogue

CHANGE OFFERED THE chance for a new beginning.

Iain Macleod stared down at the acceptance letter and the rest of the papers that he had to fill out in order to make his transfer to Hathaway House happen. He took a slow and deep measured breath.

Everybody here knew him as a class clown, somebody who threw off the problems and stresses in his life without a care. Most looked at him sideways, wondering how he managed it. But he also knew he was at the end of his rope—knew that he couldn't keep up the facade. It was time for a change, and it could only happen if he left here and went where people didn't know him. A place he could go to find the depths of his soul, to find a way to live with the future as he had it right now. Because it looked pretty shitty from where he sat.

He didn't want to hear any more about "probably never walk again" or "probably never be fully functioning in society again." Just so many damn *probablys* that he didn't even want to contemplate it.

He had both hands, and he had a sturdy back, and that was more than a lot of guys had. Iain was missing a leg, but he still had one. It was kind of shriveled and didn't do so well, but that's because he'd had a lot of muscle torn off it. He'd also had the recommended surgery to put new muscle back on, and, so far, it was an unknown as to how well that would work. He roomed with three others, and he lived with hundreds, all in the same type of nightmarish scenario that he was in. Everybody was different, and everybody was unique, and yet all so much the same.

It hurt. All of it hurt. Humor and laughter had been his shields, which might have fooled everybody else, but they weren't fooling him.

He'd gone as far as he could, staring at himself, seeing the joker and the ultimate joke that life had thrown at him. Yet he knew, if he wanted to make anything out of his world, he had to cross that abyss and had to learn to live with the best that he had, which was what that surgery had given him. To maximize this point, he needed therapy that went well past what he had access to here, and that was stupid. This was a VA hospital. He should have had the best of the best right here, but he knew from what he'd seen that he didn't. From what he'd heard about Hathaway House, he knew there was more. He'd contacted several people who had been there and had left much improved. They'd all told him the same thing.

"Go. You won't be disappointed."

Taking that chance, he'd put his John Doe on an application form, and he'd sent it off. He hadn't told anybody here, and, if he had, nobody would have been more surprised than him when he'd been accepted. Now after more paperwork, more medical appointments, and a painful transfer, maybe he'd have a chance at a new life. Or at least a chance at living the life that he'd been given as best as he could.

And really, was there more to anything in life than that?

This concludes Book 8 of Hathaway House: Heath.

Read about Iain: Hathaway House, Book 9

# Hathaway House: Iain (Book #9)

Welcome to Hathaway House, a heartwarming and sweet military romance series from USA TODAY best-selling author Dale Mayer. Here you'll meet a whole new group of friends, along with a few favorite characters from Heroes for Hire. Instead of action, you'll find emotion. Instead of suspense, you'll find healing. Instead of romance, … oh, wait. … There is romance—of course!

**_Welcome to Hathaway House. Rehab Center. Safe Haven. Second chance at life and love._**

Getting accepted to Hathaway House is the new start Iain MacLeod has been waiting for. His old VA center has put him on the road to recovery, but he's nowhere near where he wants to be. Much work remains to be done, and Iain is determined to do what's necessary to get back to full power. But he has hit the limit of his current professionals' abilities. He needs a new team. New eyes. New methods. He can only hope that Hathaway House has what he needs to keep moving forward.

Robin Carruthers works in the veterinary clinic at Hathaway House. When she connects with Iain, she's his biggest cheerleader and enjoys watching him take steps toward greater recovery. Until she realizes that, while Iain is growing in major ways, … she isn't. When traumas from her past intrude on the present, and Robin is forced to confront issues of her own, she's afraid she and Iain won't find their way back to each other again …

Find Book 9 here!

To find out more visit Dale Mayer's website.

http://smarturl.it/DMSIain

# Author's Note

Thank you for reading Heath: Hathaway House, Book 8! If you enjoyed the book, please take a moment and leave a short review.

Dear reader,

I love to hear from readers, and you can contact me at my website: www.dalemayer.com or at my Facebook author page. To be informed of new releases and special offers, sign up for my newsletter or follow me on BookBub. And if you are interested in joining Dale Mayer's Reader Group, here is the Facebook sign up page.
https://smarturl.it/DaleMayerFBGroup

Cheers,
Dale Mayer

# Get THREE Free Books Now!

Have you met the SEALS of Honor?

SEALs of Honor Books 1, 2, and 3. Follow the stories of brave, badass warriors who serve their country with honor and love their women to the limits of life and death.

Read Mason, Hawk, and Dane right now for FREE.

Go here and tell me where to send them!
http://smarturl.it/EthanBofB

# About the Author

Dale Mayer is a USA Today bestselling author best known for her Psychic Visions and Family Blood Ties series. Her contemporary romances are raw and full of passion and emotion (Second Chances, SKIN), her thrillers will keep you guessing (By Death series), and her romantic comedies will keep you giggling (It's a Dog's Life and Charmin Marvin Romantic Comedy series).

She honors the stories that come to her – and some of them are crazy and break all the rules and cross multiple genres!

To go with her fiction, she also writes nonfiction in many different fields with books available on resume writing, companion gardening and the US mortgage system. She has recently published her Career Essentials Series. All her books are available in print and ebook format.

## Connect with Dale Mayer Online

*Dale's Website – www.dalemayer.com*
*Facebook Personal – https://smarturl.it/DaleMayer*
*Instagram – https://smarturl.it/DaleMayerInstagram*
*BookBub – https://smarturl.it/DaleMayerBookbub*
*Facebook Fan Page – https://smarturl.it/DaleMayerFBFanPage*
*Goodreads – https://smarturl.it/DaleMayerGoodreads*

# Also by Dale Mayer

## Published Adult Books:

### Hathaway House
Aaron, Book 1
Brock, Book 2
Cole, Book 3
Denton, Book 4
Elliot, Book 5
Finn, Book 6
Gregory, Book 7
Heath, Book 8
Iain, Book 9

### The K9 Files
Ethan, Book 1
Pierce, Book 2
Zane, Book 3
Blaze, Book 4
Lucas, Book 5
Parker, Book 6
Carter, Book 7

### Lovely Lethal Gardens
Arsenic in the Azaleas, Book 1
Bones in the Begonias, Book 2
Corpse in the Carnations, Book 3
Daggers in the Dahlias, Book 4

Evidence in the Echinacea, Book 5
Footprints in the Ferns, Book 6
Gun in the Gardenias, Book 7
Handcuffs in the Heather, Book 8

## Psychic Vision Series
Tuesday's Child
Hide 'n Go Seek
Maddy's Floor
Garden of Sorrow
Knock Knock...
Rare Find
Eyes to the Soul
Now You See Her
Shattered
Into the Abyss
Seeds of Malice
Eye of the Falcon
Itsy-Bitsy Spider
Unmasked
Deep Beneath
From the Ashes
Psychic Visions Books 1–3
Psychic Visions Books 4–6
Psychic Visions Books 7–9

## By Death Series
Touched by Death
Haunted by Death
Chilled by Death
By Death Books 1–3

## Broken Protocols – Romantic Comedy Series
Cat's Meow
Cat's Pajamas
Cat's Cradle
Cat's Claus
Broken Protocols 1-4

## Broken and... Mending
Skin
Scars
Scales (of Justice)
Broken but... Mending 1-3

## Glory
Genesis
Tori
Celeste
Glory Trilogy

## Biker Blues
Morgan: Biker Blues, Volume 1
Cash: Biker Blues, Volume 2

## SEALs of Honor
Mason: SEALs of Honor, Book 1
Hawk: SEALs of Honor, Book 2
Dane: SEALs of Honor, Book 3
Swede: SEALs of Honor, Book 4
Shadow: SEALs of Honor, Book 5
Cooper: SEALs of Honor, Book 6
Markus: SEALs of Honor, Book 7
Evan: SEALs of Honor, Book 8
Mason's Wish: SEALs of Honor, Book 9

Chase: SEALs of Honor, Book 10

Brett: SEALs of Honor, Book 11

Devlin: SEALs of Honor, Book 12

Easton: SEALs of Honor, Book 13

Ryder: SEALs of Honor, Book 14

Macklin: SEALs of Honor, Book 15

Corey: SEALs of Honor, Book 16

Warrick: SEALs of Honor, Book 17

Tanner: SEALs of Honor, Book 18

Jackson: SEALs of Honor, Book 19

Kanen: SEALs of Honor, Book 20

Nelson: SEALs of Honor, Book 21

Taylor: SEALs of Honor, Book 22

Colton: SEALs of Honor, Book 23

SEALs of Honor, Books 1–3

SEALs of Honor, Books 4–6

SEALs of Honor, Books 7–10

SEALs of Honor, Books 11–13

SEALs of Honor, Books 14–16

SEALs of Honor, Books 17–19

## Heroes for Hire

Levi's Legend: Heroes for Hire, Book 1

Stone's Surrender: Heroes for Hire, Book 2

Merk's Mistake: Heroes for Hire, Book 3

Rhodes's Reward: Heroes for Hire, Book 4

Flynn's Firecracker: Heroes for Hire, Book 5

Logan's Light: Heroes for Hire, Book 6

Harrison's Heart: Heroes for Hire, Book 7

Saul's Sweetheart: Heroes for Hire, Book 8

Dakota's Delight: Heroes for Hire, Book 9

Michael's Mercy (Part of Sleeper SEAL Series)

Tyson's Treasure: Heroes for Hire, Book 10
Jace's Jewel: Heroes for Hire, Book 11
Rory's Rose: Heroes for Hire, Book 12
Brandon's Bliss: Heroes for Hire, Book 13
Liam's Lily: Heroes for Hire, Book 14
North's Nikki: Heroes for Hire, Book 15
Anders's Angel: Heroes for Hire, Book 16
Reyes's Raina: Heroes for Hire, Book 17
Dezi's Diamond: Heroes for Hire, Book 18
Vince's Vixen: Heroes for Hire, Book 19
Ice's Icing: Heroes for Hire, Book 20
Heroes for Hire, Books 1–3
Heroes for Hire, Books 4–6
Heroes for Hire, Books 7–9
Heroes for Hire, Books 10–12
Heroes for Hire, Books 13–15

## SEALs of Steel
Badger: SEALs of Steel, Book 1
Erick: SEALs of Steel, Book 2
Cade: SEALs of Steel, Book 3
Talon: SEALs of Steel, Book 4
Laszlo: SEALs of Steel, Book 5
Geir: SEALs of Steel, Book 6
Jager: SEALs of Steel, Book 7
The Final Reveal: SEALs of Steel, Book 8
SEALs of Steel, Books 1–4
SEALs of Steel, Books 5–8
SEALs of Steel, Books 1–8

## The Mavericks
Kerrick, Book 1
Griffin, Book 2

Jax, Book 3
Beau, Book 4
Asher, Book 5
Ryker, Book 6
Miles, Book 7
Nico, Book 8
Keane, Book 9
Lennox, Book 10
Gavin, Book 11
Shane, Book 12

## Collections
Dare to Be You…
Dare to Love…
Dare to be Strong…
RomanceX3

## Standalone Novellas
It's a Dog's Life
Riana's Revenge
Second Chances

# Published Young Adult Books:

## Family Blood Ties Series
Vampire in Denial
Vampire in Distress
Vampire in Design
Vampire in Deceit
Vampire in Defiance
Vampire in Conflict
Vampire in Chaos
Vampire in Crisis

Vampire in Control
Vampire in Charge
Family Blood Ties Set 1–3
Family Blood Ties Set 1–5
Family Blood Ties Set 4–6
Family Blood Ties Set 7–9
Sian's Solution, A Family Blood Ties Series Prequel
    Novelette

## Design series
Dangerous Designs
Deadly Designs
Darkest Designs
Design Series Trilogy

## Standalone
In Cassie's Corner
Gem Stone (a Gemma Stone Mystery)
Time Thieves

# Published Non-Fiction Books:

## Career Essentials
Career Essentials: The Résumé
Career Essentials: The Cover Letter
Career Essentials: The Interview
Career Essentials: 3 in 1

Made in the USA
Coppell, TX
20 December 2019